Lee Richardson

SUBLIMINISM
A Brief History in the Art of Being

© 2023 **Europe Books**| London
www.europebooks.co.uk | info@europebooks.co.uk

ISBN 9791220138635
First edition: May 2023

SUBLIMINISM
A Brief History in the Art of Being

The Sunshine to his candle,
the Moonlight of his rock.
For my children.

Thank you to my family,
without them none of this would have been possible.
Thank you for the love of my family,
without it none of this would be of value.

Life has been your art.
You have set yourself to music.
Your days are your sonnets.
Oscar Wilde

Michaela
with love

Chapter one
Several years ago, my mind broke.

Like a large glistening watermelon dropped onto the unforgiving marble slab it broke almost in two. Trying to recover, the sharp-edged blade of a cleaver came and shorn it into two halves. Sparkling, sweet, red meat lay open, jet-black seeds and all, lay open to the observer. The observer is me. Every so often it feels like spiny, sharp, cruel fingers poke their way into it, disturbing the lush meat laying within. I'm not wrong. Those fingers are my own. Other times it feels like the soft, caring tongue of the bee and the butterfly gratefully lapping up the juices, taking just what they need, because the creatures of the Universe are not inherently greedy, maybe a little needy, but not greedy. Greed is a construct of a self-service society bent on an envy that doesn't really exist in Nature as a conscious goal. The flower that sees a bigger flower, as far as I am aware, does not expand and entangle its roots consciously around the roots of another smaller flower. It doesn't purposely put its own bright coloured head in front of another, hoping to take its supply of water or put the other flowers' bright petals in the shade, starving it of light and food.

(Where Is My Mind – Sunday Girl) 4 060 960

There are a lot of instances in nature, it is true, that involve the patriarchal male monopolising a large portion of the females in order to ensure his own lineage. The Alpha male. Big and strong but not the only one. As far as I am aware the Greek Alphabet goes up to 24 and actually includes Pi and Chi Rho. The Universe knows it takes more than the aggressive masculine brute strength of the Lion to prevail within a society. Does the Epsilon monkey climb the highest tree in shame at his inadequacies? Perhaps, not realising, head bowed, forehead in the Sun, beautiful view of the vista before him, he has just become his own Alpha. He is the first to climb that tree the other monkeys dare not. There is an abundance of fruit up here for him. He realises he doesn't have to fight for food anymore. The biggest portion of his brain requiring him to secure a mate and hunt for food has now left him. The brain left free of its basic functions of survival! What does a brain that has nothing left to think about other than basic motor skills then think about? Does Epsilon monkey look at the Sun and the colours before him and feel a surge of something within him that can only be described as an aestheticism never before experienced by any other of the monkeys squabbling on the ground below him. Epsilon will find his mate among the horde promised to Alpha because some years later his ancestry will create an artwork history and offer an insight into his life that will be seen by the world many years later. His mate will be the one plucky enough to brave the heights of the canopy he sits beyond. She will be the one that realises that the term Alpha to Omega doesn't just apply to the males of their perfect society. She is the one that went against the grain of what is supposed to be and had a thought of what could be.

Where is Pi monkey? He is sat by the river. He gathers rocks to throw at the crocodiles that threaten his drinking point. Their bulging hungry eyes rise above the water and Pi smashes them with the rocks he has gathered. They used to be in a pile, the rocks, now they are spread out. He knows how many shots he has at the crocs before he makes his way to find more rocks to shot at the crocs that he mocks. Pi has just learnt the amount of substance he has to the actions he can take. Pi has learnt to count. Pi finds his mate. His seemingly arbitrary acts of mindless abandon save one of the females from the jaws of the hungry croc. They go off into the forest together and return sometime later. They sit side by side, with rocks spread out separately before them, she knows how to count too. Beta, Gamma and Delta sit huddled under a tree planning the overthrow of Alpha. They tend each other and bare snarling teeth at any other males that come near them. In their own way they have made a pact with each other they will not keep.

Chi and Rho are at peace with themselves and the World around them and seek to offer their good-naturedness to the despondent among the group. They have found compassion. A care for the well-being of the society. Some will respond gratefully. Others not so. Everyone needs a little, or a lot, of what Chi Rho offer - even Epsilon and Pi. Who knows, perhaps even Alpha to Delta – eventually.

(Adventure of a Lifetime – Coldplay) 1 376 869 776

And so, the Man, chained to a darkness, a material moment in the dark-space orbit of his own Universe, dark side of the Moon, what does he do? Does he learn to love himself? Not now. Not here. His heart is not for this place. His heart is the hard-closed shell of the oyster. Give it time. Time. Time. The brain seeing that the heart, at this moment in time, is too weak and vulnerable to take on the assault he will have to endure, closes, knowing it has just become the one responsible for the survival of the vehicle it occupies. The Man, with his brain at the helm becomes a colder, more aloof representation of himself.

"How do you talk to him?" They ask. The wife replies: "Just don't!" They don't know and I am not telling them I am already exhausted from talking to myself. The brain closed prematurely with fingers still in there poking and prodding the deepest reaches. They press buttons that access every memory that would justify his arrival and current habitation of this place. There are many, even actions that would seem insignificant to others, explode in his mind like loud bright fireworks. His imagination is on fire and his failings epic. He is drowning. Looking up from the depths at his own reflection he pleads for help. The man, blinking, looks to his right and sees the electric traces of a small birdlike shape soar towards him on brightly coloured currents and straight into him. He looks up at the ceiling and opens his mouth and ash-like, burnt paper type objects, saunter into the air and disappear. This is the one and only time this happens to him, but not the only time his imagination would take on the form of an entity that was not his own. (And at this particular moment in space realises the irony of working in an area nicknamed the 'Green Mile.') His mind has just discovered how to get through this. His reflection has just pulled him from the water.

(The Sound of Silence [Electric Version] – Simon & Garfunkel) 209 186

Chapter Two
A couple of years ago, my heart re-opened like a flower.

Its petals opened like those of arms outstretched to the Divine. The oyster, open slightly, emits a radiant blue glow within. The man feels a love raging within him neglected for a time. A fire burning with an intensity long since forgotten. He wants to shout it, scream it, create a beauty of light so wonderful that its luminescent glow can be seen by even the blind. But he is not perfect and so he is fearful. There is a reason. Those that carry a light for others to live in, enjoy, harbour in safety in, are closer to the unseen and unknown body of darkness than anybody else. A couple of years ago, my heart re-opened like a flower.

(I See You – Leona Lewis) 32 536 605

The harsh Winter has forced the tribe to move from the open lands of their current home. Winds chill them to the bones through their thick animal skins, so the tribe tread through heavy snow underfoot searching for a relief. They have fire but are unable to keep it aflame in the conditions. They come across a mountain that appears to have a hole carved into its face. The tribe exchange looks from one to another, until one of the group takes hold of a lighted torch, drops to his knees and shuffles his way through the hole into a large, darkened space. He is fearful, he does not know what could be in here lurking in the dark, but also knows that the existence of his tribe relies on their ability to escape the harsh outside conditions and his ability to brave the unknown to secure their shelter. He has fears but has faith in something far and above his own safety. He leaves a torch propped on a rock close to the entrance of the cave and ushers for them to enter. Hesitantly, one by one they enter. He lights a second torch and moves further into the cave, signalling for the others to remain close to the torch and the light provided. He moves purposefully but extremely cautiously around the walls of the cave, propping up torches and lighting new ones before moving on.

(Cavatina – The Deer Hunter) 14 956 182

Chapter Three
Kind words, positive vibes and benevolent gestures encourage most souls to strive to excel.

Cruel words, negative vibes and bad intentions sometimes encourage a soul to strive to excel. That is the a-ha moment! It is not the external that really encourages a soul to strive – it certainly helps, but it is not dependant on it either. The heart, the soul, lit with passion doesn't need the endorsement of riches or popularity. The passionate heart can live without the wild boar of wealth. The cold fizzing judgemental pop of the spotlight. Watch them hunt the animal. A wedge of flat dead lifeless eyes lined in pockets. Pinch yourself. Yes, it's still you. Knock on the thick bolted door on the forehead. Opens. Shit! I still feel the same but in a bigger space! The leaf that drops from the tree is still the same leaf that floats merrily down the stream... Isn't it? See them squint at the harsh light. Eyes on you like tiny splinters of green glass.

It is a singular love, a passion, an expression sometimes buried deep within your very core. It shouts; its voice starts as a whisper at cellular level, which passes its message on through the cells until the voice is heard within you like the incessant bang of the snare. And it fizzes, and fizzles and bubbles until it tries to blow the top off the bottle. Is it the finest champagne or the cheapest fizzy pop? Only time will tell.

(Thunder in My Heart – Meck Feat Leo Sayer) 3 299 587

The artist pushes aside a single cover and jumps from his straw mattress. He already feels like he's wasted enough time on the three hours' sleep he didn't actually have. When he did lose consciousness, briefly, he was doing what he was about to go and do. Such a lovely dream. Such a short and sumptuous life! The Riviera Sun turns the profile of the horizon into red burning embers. He grabs a half-eaten crusted, stale - loaf of bread and a wedge of cheese adorned with teeth-marks. Lazy dentures. He packs them in a handkerchief and stuffs them into the pocket of the pants he slept in. His ragged, paint-smudged shirt hangs off his back and is buttoned two-up; the creases upon it, testimony to a frustrated and movemental, (lack of) sleep! He hurriedly grabs the paraphernalia of his personal ecstasy and heads out. The Sun hits his face and makes his eyes close as if they were trying to escape the orange flames of his beard and hair. He runs to his destination like the bull charging the matador. "Must get the right light! Must get the right light!" He pulls out a palette covered in every hue of yellow and blue. A small knob of black paint and white paint sit in tandem like Yin and Yang. The artist has no idea how great he is… What he does know: "What is done in love is done well."

(Vincent – Don McClean) 60 690 825

The shutters to his bedroom roll up slowly, but noise-lessly, to reveal a semi-circular golden orb, fiery fingers pulling itself up over the Sea. The sun rays knock on his eyelids. He was already awake; he just hadn't opened his eyes yet. His therapist told him he needed to relax more to lower his blood pressure. She told him he had to consciously slow down, instead of charging into every-thing; take a moment, just a moment, to sit or lay and relax. He would learn to relax more, ease his stress, the more he got used to doing this small exercise daily. Now he wakes 10 minutes earlier every day! He would do as she said, he wants to live forever – so long as it fits into his schedule. So, he rose up from plush pillows and pushes aside satin sheets from silk pyjamas. He feels an electric charge; it's just the friction. He steps into slippers and idles to the window, stretching, as he watches the Sun rise up from the sea, a view the proper-ty affords. A magical scene of Nature unfolds before his eager eyes. He doesn't see the Sun. He sees a timepiece. The Hong Kong Exchange has just closed. After being served a breakfast that he will barely touch the morning paper will tell him whether his children have multiplied. Sat huddled in a vault together what else is there for them to do? Sometimes, some of the lucky ones find their way out of the bulging vault and out into the World.

(Morning Mood – Edvard Grieg) 7 744 134

The same Sunshine streams through the blinds of the hospital and stripes the young woman asleep fully clothed on the bed. Her only state of undress are her sandals which lay on top of each other beside the bed. Her feet bare the flaking marks of nail polish applied three weeks earlier. She sleeps because she has been awake all night and the man, who arrived an hour earlier didn't wake her. He is asleep in a chair by the window, his leg flapping over one of the arms of the chairs. He hasn't bothered to take off his muddy work boots; he is exhausted from another twelve-hour shift. Hospital treatment is expensive. He hasn't even bothered to wash his face, and the muck ingrained upon it is punctuated by a couple of clean trails running from his eyes. The little girl is sat upright in bed; her sparkling eyes of the purest azure blue are focused on a picture she is drawing. Her mother wakes with a start and rubs her tired eyes.

"Why didn't you wake me, Honey?"

"Cos you looked so peaceful, Mommy!"

The woman affectionately squeezes her daughters' forearm and rubs it before sitting up.

"What are you drawing?"

The girl turns her picture around to reveal a waxen yellow ball sat atop a shimmering blue horizon.

"I wish I could visit the sea again…"

(Somewhere Over the Rainbow – Israel 'IZ') 1 263 882 228

Chapter Four

Several years ago, I began seeing signs and synchro-nicities in everything.

In the darkness the mind played tricks. No longer was an image, a word, a metaphor just that. It took on a depth never previously experienced. An Eagle could be the savage tormentor of a chained-up Prometheus or the soft winged saviour of the Angel in Lady in the Water depending on my mood.

In here, in the darkness, my mood was rarely of a higher vibrational state and as a consequence I became my own torturer. Everything I had ever done became magnified. I presented to myself a narrative that wasn't true or at least disproportional to the action. When it was bad, it was really bad. When it was better, I could be anything I wanted to be and sometimes the external world compromised this opinion.

(Lost Cause – Billie Eilish) 100 109 423

The Man sat in a white plastic bucket chair in the centre of the room in his issued sweatpants and burgun-dy jumper; legs pushed out in front of him and crossed at the ankles. His eyes were fixated on the heavy green door, but his mind was elsewhere. A hatch opened and a nurse announced: "Medication." No emotion, just a statement of fact. The Man raised himself and took the folded piece of paper left on the ledge of the door. The hatch was now closed, and he heard the nurse repeat the process to the room next door. He opened up the paper to reveal a small pill which slid from view and into the infinity of his room. "Shit!" He took a cursory look around his vicinity before dropping to hands and knees in search of the pill. Inching his way around the brightly lit room he couldn't find it anywhere. He pressed the attention bell on his wall and re-seated himself in the bucket chair. Slouched, he waited. Some minutes later the harassed face of the nurse returned.

"What's wrong!?" He moved to the hatch.

"I've dropped my pill on the floor…"

"Well, look for it!"

"I have. I've searched the room…" She tuts.

"You'll have to wait till I can get hold of an Officer!"

Hatch closes. Man returns to the bucket chair in his sparse brightly lit room of green and angry grey. For some reason he is not laying on his bed watching the TV. Maybe it was sometime after he had either asked an Officer to remove his TV one afternoon or the other time when he threw his TV against a wall or maybe it was because tonight… Sometime later, nothing was ever quick here, the nurse returned and looked through the hatch before the exaggerated metallic click of locks went through their processes before revealing the nurse in the doorway in blue, shrouded on either side by two Officers like black wings. The Man raised himself and began explaining what had happened and why he was disturbing her from her film or magazine or whatever it was they were disturbed from on a night that pissed them off so much. He was talking to the nurse, but he was focusing on the Officers, trying to establish eye contact. Neither gave him any, in fact, it looked as if their life depended on them avoiding it. He tried, he tried, but they just wouldn't. The nurse was pissed off but gave him a pill anyway; and remained there whilst he took it. He swallowed and pulled up his tongue and once again tried to establish an eye connection with the Officers before they left. Why? Because tonight he was Ghost Rider. They refused. The Man, Ghost Rider, returned to his bucket chair and waited for the medication to kick in. Some years later, the Man, mended from the dark place was walking home from work and had a conversation with his wife all the way home. The journey was an hour long. It was the longest and probably most candid exchange either one of them had ever had. But he had walked home alone.

(Bad Guy – Billie Eilish) 1 217 097 175

Epsilon felt the first spots of rain and moved beneath a canopy of leaves further down the tree where his mate sat. She hadn't been to the top of the tree for a while, she was heavily pregnant. She looked at him a little sadly and he offered his arm which interlocked with hers. He looked into her eyes. He knew she was right. It wasn't a bitter pill for him to swallow; he was well aware of his responsibilities as a father. He moved behind her and started grooming her back. In the morning they would head off on down to the bottom of the tree.

(Left to My Own Devices – Pet Shop Boys) 5 959 958

At the bottom of the tree Alpha is being groomed by a couple of his harem; another couple of them are nearby tending Alpha's children. There is a perfectly calm air of dominating serenity until another male wanders into their circle, their bubble. Alpha starts hollering loudly and in exaggerated fashion, baring teeth, as the other male freezes like a statue. He pushes one of his females aside and on hands and feet tears towards the male still hollering loudly before stopping in front and then circling the unfortunate trespasser. Alpha's children are hollering too and one of them is doing somersaults in a frenzy. The bravest and clearly the next generation Alpha launches towards the male and climbs up his arm before planting a slap on the top of the top of the male's head. Alpha presents himself in front of the stunned monkey and presents his arm out to him, palm faced upwards. The trespasser bows his head and rubs it along the knuckles of Alpha before moving away. Alpha returns to his leafy throne before little Alpha runs and jumps and clutches onto the neck of his father. Order is restored in Treetopia.

(A Town Called Malice – The Jam) 20 782 295

The old man is writing a sermon. He doesn't know that one day he will figure in the musings of an aspiring artist because he believes that the World will end this year; or rather the world as we know it. It is the year of our Lord 1666. The old man's son strides confidently through the narrow-cobbled streets of London despite the plague that has ravaged the city. His expensive boots ring noisily in the cloying streets and echo up and out into the London air beyond the busy 3-storey wooden buildings that loom over him on both sides. He is unconcerned. Alive and imbued with a Faith in his own mortality that has been within him since he was a child. Blessed with a confidence and brazenness that education and intelligence have afforded him. He turns a corner and into a house where an old man looks up from the candle-light and puts down his quill. His son sits at the table opposite and lights another candle. "Father." They talk long into the night. His father explains that soon his time of writing sermons will be over: "... Plague, war, this is just the beginning, my boy, it is written! Novus. Innovatio!" His son takes his father's hand, who offers him a grateful smile. The son has listened to his father all of his life about the manoeuvrings of God. The man loves his father, and he does believe in God and Jesus Christ he just believes they move in a slightly different way. As he walks back home through the narrow wooden streets he is thinking about his next venture. "Supply and demand..." He passes a man with a flaming torch chasing a rat that scurries away. Father may be right, he thinks, this place is a tinder box waiting to happen.

(Opportunities – Pet Shop Boys) 6 259 764

He lay on his bed looking at the ceiling. His coffee was going cold on the bedside table. His laptop was flicked open on an astrological website. The little tabs at the top of the screen were mainly wiki sites. He was researching something historical, trying to read between the lines of the words of presented fact. He wasn't a conspiracy theorist he just didn't take everything at face value. If the top echelons of society were proven liars where did the truth actually lay? The truth lay in what it is you actually know he thought to himself. He was counting in his head. Birth dates. His first fiancé, his second fiancé and his wife – all the girls he had been in a committed relationship with – all had a numerological value of 11! Is that strange? He thought it a little. He was a four. Why is four the only number that has two different spellings?

(One and One – Robert Miles) 4 502 307

He delved further; his brows furrowed in concentration. In this equation he discarded his first fiancé - the first 11 in the sequence – for he had had no children with her. He totted up the numbers $38 + 39 = 77$ second fiancé and eldest daughter; $29 + 24 + 24 = 77$ wife and twins. He recalculated, fuck off! He rose up and took his notebook and pen and separated the calculations with a line.

$7 + 7 = 14 = 5$
$7 + 7 = 14 = 5$
$77 + 77 = 154 +$ (My number) $31 = 185$
$185 = 14 = 5$

Okay, the 555 is quite significant probably, but the mind of the man focuses on something different because it is personal to him. $14 + 14 + 14 = 42$! Anyone who has read Hitchhikers Guide to the Galaxy knows the significance of 42 and the man has just realised that the answer to his own personal Universe, though he already knew it, is all there in numbers. Families! (Pythagorean: $38 = 11$) (Gematria: 402)

(1999 – Binary Finary) 400 133

Chapter Five
Every day we interact and connect.

Every day we interact and connect, sometimes, maybe just once in a lifetime – perhaps never at all – we come across an interaction, a connection that sets off a spark within us. A spark that lights the forest of our imagination and sets it ablaze with ferocious and unstoppable force.

(Unstoppable - Sia 'Lucy') 1 977 703

Epsilon and his mate had moved off the tree. Now that they were in the shaded canopy of the forest floor, sometimes, he missed the warmth of the Sun, the bright light and colours it displayed from his vantage point at the top of the world. He missed the glimmering silver light of the Moon as it cast its light and shadows on the dark plain of the world below him. Every so often when his mate slept, her child, his child, clinging to her neck in a scene of serene and perfect bliss he would climb the top of the tree, just for a while, making sure he was back before they awoke.

(Coming Around Again – Carly Simon) 27 174 478

She was crying on the hospital phone. A couple walked past her and as she turned to look at them, they averted their eyes. Crying in a hospital was no spectator sport.

"Please, Dad! You need to speak to him... Come and see her. She misses her Grandad."

The woman's father put down his landline phone on a table next to the armchair he sat in. He sat looking into space. A glare focused on the ochre-stained décor of his living room. A tear fell without his knowledge or acknowledgement of it. Another fell, follow my leader, down his face and onto the pale blue of an open shirt. "I can't," he whispered to himself, and he refused to look anywhere but on a spot on the wall before him. "I can't!" He said aloud angrily and when he caught sight of her on a picture on the mantelpiece the avalanche of tears fell from his rigid proud body.

(When You Tell Me That You Love Me – Diana Ross) 1 000 070

The old man was finishing his sermon. The four Empires of man were at an end and God would show his might, his anger, his majesty with fire and brimstone before the Fifth Monarchy, the Kingdom and Kingship of Jesus Christ, will rule over the world. The hundred or so that were there listened intently to the charismatic impassioned little man except for a couple of the Landoners that were making their departure. "Fuckin' crazy old coot!" One of them announced to the other huddled together in a shared joke as they began to walk away. Their merriment didn't last long as a tall hawk-like figure of a man dressed all in black finery stepped in front of them. They were about to protest. They even thought about getting aggressive until they looked into the dark stone eyes of the man. They separated and averted their eyes with humility. "Excuse us, Sir." The man in black looked from the little men and back up to his father who was gathering up his sermon papers to a round of applause.

(Fire – Arthur Brown) 2 581 400

Epsilon and his family were by the river, drinking, then moving away. From where they sat, they watched as Pi returned with the rocks he had gathered and sat closer to the river than any of the others. He watched transfixed as Pi dropped the rocks in front of himself and separated them in the sand. Epsilon moved over to where Pi sat, and they interacted before Pi offered Epsilon one of the rocks he had gathered. Epsilon returned to where his family sat in the sand and his mate groomed him as he examined the stone. He turned it, moved it from hand to hand and traced his fingers along its edges. He let out a little hoot when he realised that the sharpness of the rock had cut his finger and droplets of blood fell onto the sand before him, as did the rock that he had held, making an impression in the sand that, when removed, looked like the ball of the Sun that he missed. With the rock he began to make marks in the sand.

(Circle in the Sand – Belinda Carlisle) 646 354

Two of the tribe were fighting over a freshly slain piece of meat in the cave they now inhabited. He watched on as they tussled. He felt no need to get involved. He had a comfortable spot by the fire and a portion of the spoils that lay content in his belly. He had everything he needed. As they wrestled over a slab of the meat, each one gripping to it like tug of war the meat left both their hands and landed with a schlop against the cave wall before sliding down leaving a red stain on the wall as it dropped. One grabbed the prize and raced off into a dark corner of the cave feeding hungrily. He looked at the stain and moved away from the fire and traced his fingers in the blood, making lines that came out from the splodge.

(Two Tribes – Frankie Goes to Hollywood) 438 631

Chapter Six

Several months before my mind broke, my temper snapped and smashed the fabric of my normal existence to smithereens.

Like the cold, hard, unfeeling metal of the ice-pick through the brittle but yielding ice. Like the non-conscious bubbling spew of the molten lava over the open mouth of the volcano. Wounds and pride left unattended, words left unsaid, in my case, were like the open cracks in the Earth and the molten lava came, both hot and as cold as liquid ice. Is this what happens to the stoic of heart, the feeling suppressor? Lives each day like the rock; expressionless, seemingly passionless, unaware that beneath the atomic fibres a flame is emerging, building - waiting for an outlet, a release - and the rock cracks and the flames pour out with a wild, untamed savagery that had never before been perceived or even conceived within his core. The seed, accepting but nevertheless assailed by the wind, landed and refused to fly anymore, dug in, took root. When we crack, what will we find? I found mine, to my own detriment and every other person involved. I ruined lives. To some on a practical material level. To others, even though I can only speak for myself - because my own mind, heart and soul is all I know - on a deeper level. I spun the barrel of the Russian Roulette revolver of fate and found the one remaining bullet. When I cracked and wanted to find the warm sunshine of forgiveness and love beneath the surface of the stone, I found me; or rather a version of me which I didn't like.

(Skyfall – Adele) 508 069 433

Chi and Rho were tending the group with their per-petual warmth and compassion. What began as a few males in the gathering had now grown to include fe-males as well; the females that had managed to avoid the clutches of Alpha… And then Beta and so on. There was a serenity in this community. A something else that couldn't normally be found in the everyday lives of these creatures. They were at peace.

(Halo – Beyonce) 1 338 982 152

The Man, stood on the doorstep of the house he shared with two others, flicked his cigarette, and placed on his mask. The taxi had arrived and not a moment too soon because given that he had to make a stop off, he was already going to be ten minutes late for his Satur-day morning shift. He jumped in the taxi: "Can you stop at a cash machine please mate?" The taxi driver nodded his begrudging consent and reversed the taxi before he headed to the end of the long street that led onto the spine-road of the town. The main hub of the Littletropo-lis. It was winter but temperate. Morning but dark. "There's one just here mate!" The road was empty. Nothing open. Nobody about. "Won't be a second." The man placed his card into the machine and punched in his digits, opting to take out the remainder of his wages un-til pay day in a few days' time. He looked around as the machine processed his request.

(Where Is My Mind [Fight Club] – Pixies) 98 912 061

The drug addicts or 'smack heads' as they would be affectionately termed in this town, had had a good time. Plenty of self-abuse and debasement had filled and fuelled their night. Now, it was morning, and they should have been heading home. Mornings were for the people. Mornings were for the clockwork. The idiots that relied on a job to pay their way through their boring and mundane – their miserable life of sobriety. They spotted one such idiot at the cash machine twenty yards further up. The big one, big as in stocky, said to the other bigger one, big as in tall: "You got any left?"

The tall one nodded his sweaty mucky head. "Yeah, I got a bitta coke..."

The stocky one: "You got this? I'm on license remember!"

The taller, looked towards the Man, who was probably fully a foot shorter, and had just clocked them walking towards him, smirked: "Piece a piss mate!"

(Mile End – Pulp) 2 907 756

The Man clocked them coming towards him and initially thought they were drinkers, drunkards even, making their way home from a lock-in or some party. He automatically looked at the taxi to assure himself it was still there but from its short distance away he couldn't make out the taxi driver; whether the driver had noticed the men looming towards him and even if the taxi driver could see him from his position a small distance away as he waited at the machine which was whirring through its time-consuming procedure. He mentally prepared himself for trouble and when they were feet away, he knew he was going to get it. If they were drunks, he would have expected a bit of verbal. At worst, a punch. When he saw the rolling eyes of the taller of the two, he remained within him a heavy sunken sigh: "Smackheads! I fuckin hate smackheads!" The taller of the two joined him on his right side, the stocky one moved behind him and to his left. He noticed that the latter, as far as smackheads go, looked quite respectably clean. Clean shaven head and face. Decent clothes. Probably the dealer. The taller pulled a bag of white powder out of his grey tracksuit bottoms and pushed it into the face of the Man as he anxiously awaited the arrival of the last of his wages to be dispensed from the machine. The beeps were going.

"Here mate, d'ya do coke? D'ya want some coke?"

The Man looked at him, both hands on either side of the cash dispenser: "I don't do it, mate…"

"Here, look at the size of it mate. Look mate!"

"I don't do it and I'm on my way to work."

The beeps ended and that is when the taller struck. He attempted to push the Man away, to the side of the cash machine as the little slot opened to reveal a small bundle of crisp notes. The Man, however, had sensed it, anticipated the attack coming and held firm, pushing his right elbow under the neck of the grappling smackhead. As the slot opened, he grabbed every single note with his left hand, before feeling the force of gravity topple him backwards and onto the taller one. He looked at the stationary taxi as he attempted to re-orientate himself. No! No movement, no sound. 'He can't see you. You're on your own, son!' His left hand hit the pavement, notes clutched in his fingers like a crisp packet, and he realised that his jaw was up. He waited and waited for the dislocating boot to his face from the stocky one that didn't come and so fought on with right hand before his would-be mugger moved swiftly backwards onto his feet and away like the clappers. The Man got to his feet and counted his money before climbing back into the taxi. He breathed a sigh of relief.

"Did they get anything?" The man looked coldly into the eyes of the taxi driver. "Did they fuck!"

The Man rang the police when he got to work – 20 minutes late. They took details and said they would be round later that day. The police never showed.

(Born Slippy [Trainspotting] – Underworld) 19 464 792

The police were there in minutes. The Man stood in his kitchen by the door to the living room with nowhere left to go. A caged animal. He knew it when he saw the bright lights pass the front room window and dance like bobbing shooting stars through the pane glass of the back door window. His wife was stood by the back door, awakened by the drama which had unfolded just minutes before, and took a step backwards as the door opened. He watched as the black uniforms cautiously entered his home; weapons drew upon him. He looked down to see three red spots splayed across his chest.

They may have said something, but it didn't register. He did hear his wife's warning tone: "Babe!" He turned around and faced his living room. It would be the last time he would ever see his home again. Within seconds of turning, he was on the floor and being bent like a pipe cleaner. Arms, knees and elbows all over his body and head as if he was a wrestling mat. He was marched unceremoniously into the back of a waiting van and on the journey, the ferryboat of his personal hell, the gravity of his actions hit home, and he wept like a new-born. He was placed in a local holding cell for approximately 36 hours before he had any real contact with the outside world. By then the cracked magnolia of the sills in the cell were presenting to him a storybook of pictures. It is amazing what the mind begins to perceive when left completely and utterly to its own devices. They told him he was going to be interviewed soon and could then make a telephone call and that if he decided, he could have a solicitor to accompany him but that would extend the time. They appeared to deem the very idea of the Man having a solicitor an inconvenience. The Man naïve to the ways and operations of social justice opted to just get the interview over with - without a solicitor. He really wanted to hear the voice of someone who loved him at this point and longed for his phone call.

(Titanium – Sia) 1 471 581 602

Some months later as he walked side by side with the solicitor that was about to represent him in court the Man asked a question that had dogged him for some time.

"If I'd have gone into interview with a solicitor, would I be facing less time than I currently face?"

The solicitor sighed and said loftily: "Some of the things you said in interview you wouldn't have said with a solicitor present. So, probably yes."

When he weighed up this sum with the fact that the arresting officers had made statements that he was going to resist arrest, which in all honesty had never entered the head of the Man, the equation that he came up with was that the safe staid uniform of the police were cast out, wrenched away, from the Venn diagram of his personal respect.

(I Fought the Law – The Clash) 20 657 190

The Grandad woke in his armchair with the half empty bottle of scotch laying horizontally upon his lap. He yawned, rubbed his eyes and made his way into the bathroom where he swilled his face. Still dressed in the black attire of yesterday's proceedings, he decided to walk off his hangover. He didn't bother to straighten his black woollen tie that hung loosely around his neck. He was past caring about such vanities. He walked in a daze. One block. Two blocks. Before he knew it, he was in the centre of town and at a crossing where a big gleaming silver sign announced the 30-storey building: 'CATHCART INDUSTRIES.' He took a seat on a bench opposite and watched as the hustle and bustle of people came and went from the immaculate building. He didn't know how long he sat there waiting, watching, getting more and more vexed before he entered the building. He moved surreptitiously with a couple of suits that made their way past the security station, who were busy with a couple of visitors, and to the stairs. When out of view of security he vaulted the steps two at a time. He was heading for the top floor and his adrenalin got him there in no time. When he reached the top floor, he straightened his tie and strode confidently towards the receptionist desk. She eyed him suspiciously and was about to say something when he pronounced loudly: "Mr Cathcart is expecting me." Before saying under his breath. "Oh, is he fuckin expecting me."

"Sir, sir, you can't..." Panicked the receptionist.

But he was away and gone and pushed open the door with plaque upon its surface: 'Adam Cathcart.' Adam Cathcart was sat in his luxurious office on his phone when he entered.

"Heartless bastard," the intruder shouted before running towards the immaculately suited entrepreneur. Adam moved backwards on the wheels of his chair as the man approached but not quick enough to avoid the sharp sting of a blow to his lip. Immediately he tasted the copper tang of blood and tried to get to his feet before feeling another blow glance across his temple that sent him sprawling across his desk. A silver gilt picture frame fell from the desk and the glass smashed on the floor. The man moved behind him and placed a strong forearm across Adam's neck before a burly mass of security pulled the man off. "Goddamn Sonofabitch. You Sonofabitch!" The man hurled as he was dragged backwards and away from the bleeding executive.

Moments later a couple of police officers entered the office with the frantic receptionist behind them. They helped subdue the raging man and get him into a chair on the far side of the room as far away from Adam Cathcart as possible. Adam was impassively wiping his lip with a handkerchief from his top pocket and looking at the man when one of the officers was reaching for his handcuffs.

"There's no need for that Officer," Adam called out. "He's my brother. He's just lost his mother. My security will take it from here."

"If you're sure Mr Cathcart, Sir."

The other officer put away his handcuffs and addressed the intruder. "You're a lucky man!" The officers left moments before security bundled the man down the stairs and out onto the street. Adam picked up the photograph that had fell to the floor. The picture, in black and white, showed a small boy in shorts smiling awkwardly at the camera with his hand upon the back of a woman focused and smiling at a baby perched in her arms.

(Lorde – Royals) 858 025 537

He picked the liveliest and lowliest of alehouses in London for the meeting. That way no-one would be able to hear what was being discussed and none of his usual contacts would ever see him here. He was in his usual black attire and the ragamuffins that sat around the table with him listened on intently. The charismatic man finished his ale and pulled out from his overcoat a velvet purse and presented it in front of the most pugnacious looking of the crew. The man was about to snatch away the purse when the man placed a black stick, silver tipped, upon it: "You know where?"

"Paddin Layne, sir... Paddin Layne!"

(The Prodigy - Firestarter) 138 452 2613}

Chapter Seven

Grief, it's like grief. Knowing there is nothing in the world you can do about it but just hope and pray that the pain of it will diminish and that normality will one day return.

He sat in the dock listening to the Judge sum up. It wasn't looking particularly promising even though the man was praised for his early plea of guilty and his previously spotless record with the judicial system. He heard the words severity and 9-16 years mentioned and the tops of his hands began to sweat. He was a passenger, in his lovely court suit, sat in the hearse on the way to his own funeral. He looked over to where his cortege sat, melancholy, quietly and soberly depressed. "However," the Judge continued. No more talking give me a figure to work with! "5 years..." The female court official came over to where he still stood. "Come on, son." The man was lowered, lower, lower. The cortege dropped white roses on the veneer of the coffin that held his cold, dead, corpse. "Till we meet again, my love." They whisper, and the Man is gone.

(Adagio in G – Albinoni) 5 552 601

The Boy is fourteen and his dealings with death are rudimentary. He has never been to a funeral and though relatives he barely knew had died, undoubtedly, in his years of existence, the truth of it all had always been shielded from him. This death they couldn't shield from him because it was his cousin and he was only a year, possibly two, older than him and he has known him, despite the geographical location, all of his life. He's not sure how to feel. Though he feels 'knowledgeable' he doesn't really know anything yet. He stands in a suit next to his old man, not his old man his father, though he is here, but with his grandad. He looks up at the old man, because he isn't as tall as him yet and sees the old oak of a man shedding acorns. He has never, ever, seen this before and he never sees it again. Tears cascading down his face like a waterfall plummeting down old rocks as the procession stands and a sweet song begins to play. Now the Boy feels something but doesn't know what. He looks again at the oak unaware that by the time he is 18 he will be more familiar with death than many his age and will eventually say goodbye to the man that stands crying tears of immortal essence to the short stays of mortal presence. His cousin, it turned out, had had something in his toe from a baby that had spread or moved up to his heart. Fate written? Isn't it all! The only certain final chapter of the human being is that they will be a human no more. Atropos always ready to cut the string when it is time. All we can hope for is that Lachesis has made it long enough to accomplish what is needed to be accomplished in this lifetime. The Boy knows little of this and leaves the church with the rest of the procession. The only reality is that his cousin has died and the fresh mound of earth protruding from the ground will sink and flatten but never leave like the raw emotions of the people that surround it today.

A year later the Boy stays at his Nana and Grampy's house in the bed that used to be occupied by his cousin. He wakes really early in the morning, itching, and removes the covers to reveal chicken pox spots all over his legs and stomach. He knows that is what they are because he has already had the malady twice in his lifetime. He curses his luck and goes back to sleep. When he awakes a few hours later there is nothing to be seen. Not one single spot!

(Cherish – Kool and the Gang) 83 044 710

Brian Cathcart rose first to the haunting voice of Edith Piaf ringing through the cosy church. The small congregation sombrely followed. He felt a hand on the small of his back as he exited the building, squinting as the sunlight addressed his eyes.

"You okay, Dad?" The man reached into his top pocket and took out a pair of sunglasses before loosening his black woollen tie.

"He didn't show! His own Mother and he didn't show..." he muttered distractedly. He looked at his daughter and she gave him a sympathetic smile. "She made me promise, promise," he pronounced this angrily, "to her last breath that I would make it up with him. Do you know what, Sweetheart? If he had showed today, I had resolved to make the effort with him. Forget the past. Bury it with her. But..." He shook his head as they walked towards the Cemetery.

"Too much, too much. You coming back to the house after? You know I'm no culinary genius, but I've laid on a plate or two."

"I can't." Hand on small of his back. "I've got to get back to the hospital... Will you be okay?"

"Don't you worry about your old man. How is Princess?"

"Fighting!" The tears appeared and Brian Cathcart hugged his daughter.

"Come on. Let's go and say goodbye to Nan..."

(Edith Piaf – Non je ne Regrette Rien) 87 955 515

He didn't know how he was going to get through today. It was his fourth funeral in three days and the drink consumed at each one lay like a thick mist of sweat beneath his crisp white shirt. This one, more than any of the others, he had to be strong. Super strong. He was carrying the coffin. He did well. He held his teenage emotions in check throughout the service. "Right. You two at the back, put your arms together at the shoulder like this, link shoulders. The coffin will sit in between. Ready? One, two, three, up..." They place the coffin in the back of the hearse amongst an array of colour. Flowers of every description and type arranged in letters. "Son." "Brother." "Friend." "Micky." The four teenage boys jump into a car and follow the hearse to the Cemetery a couple of miles away. The turnout was massive, and they all watch and wait around the burial plot as the four boys carry their friend, their brother, to his final resting place. People have come from miles away to be here, and he offers one such person a smile of gratitude as he walks past her. He walks past his mother and up to the weeping throng. He is lowered down into the earth, and a young girl falls to her knees crying as she drops earth and a rose onto the coffin. Nobody is judging, everyone is sympathetic. It is a sad, sad waste of boy full of life and promise. One of God's finest. The teenage boy drops earth and a rose onto the coffin and looks at the granite black shiny tombstone, inscribed with a phrase in quotation marks: "Amigos Siempre". He touches the stone as he walks past and moves on.

"Till we meet again, Brother."

He sees his mother by the gates and heads into her arms and breaks down like a falling dam.

(He Ain't Heavy - The Hollies) 1 077 422

The artist stumbled over the threshold to the Inn, his red hair, beard, and face drenched in sweat, and headed for the stairs clutching his stomach. He is spotted by the Innkeeper.

"Monsieur! Monsieur! Are you okay?"

The artist stops briefly. "I just need to get to my room! Just need to… Rest." The artist opens the door to his room and drops heavily onto his mattress and curls into a ball groaning in pain. The Innkeeper disturbed by the noise echoing from the room, enters frantically.

"Monsieur! What is wrong? Are you sick?"

The artist opens up his blood-stained shirt to reveal a gaping bullet wound. "It is my body, my body," he says deliriously before passing out.

Over the next couple of days, the wound is dressed, and the artist falls in and out of consciousness. On the second day his brother is sat by his bedside.

"I want to go." The artist says patting his brother's hand. "I want to go." He leaves this world moments later. At the funeral, his distraught brother is stopped by an artist friend of his brother. "He (his work) was never appreciated in this lifetime. Perhaps in the next, my friend, perhaps in the next!"

(Whiter Shade of Pale – Procol Harum) 115 642 716

Jessica sits up in bed with a serious expression on her face. Her mother is sat by her bedside still dressed in the black attire from the funeral earlier.
"Mommy? Are you scared of dying?"
The woman sits up a little taken aback by the question. "No, Honeysuckle. No, I'm not." (What she doesn't say: there are some things in a mother's life more dreaded than her own mortality.)

"Do you believe in Heaven?"

"Of course, my Angel." (Because where do all the beautiful creatures go? Because if I don't, I'll fall apart at the seams.)

"I love you, Mommy."

The woman raises from her chair and squeezes her daughter tightly. "I love you, Honeysuckle." ("More than I can bear. More than I can bear.")

(Beethoven – Moonlight Sonata) 9 838 253

Chapter Eight

There is a love within a human that would stop bullets; shield from the sharp point of the sword; instil a fear and a faith of equal measure so intense we wonder how our weak meagre bodies can hold onto it.

Nothing prepares us for the birth of a child. Nothing before. Nothing in-between. When I looked down into her blue dewy eyes, as deep as the Ocean, but with an innocence so pure, so fragile, it made me feel like King Kong with a heart like a soft summer breeze and as stout and strong as Ayers Rock. There were people in life I would gladly take a bullet for, and I was consciously aware of it.

On this day I met the person who made the consciousness of the fact a formality, a duty. It was already ingrained in my unconscious. I had sat in this room for ten, thirty, then sixty minutes before the bundle was presented to me and lay in my arms like a rare bird's egg. An hour before there was a panicked scene of shapes moving rapidly before his eyes. "No heartbeat! We have to get her down for C section. Now!" Her mother was out of it, epidural, gas and air, her father stood helpless before being led and quickly ushered into an empty room where he was joined by his partner's stepmother. Not much was said between us that I can remember. I'm sure she was reassuring me but the drawn-out ticking of the clock on the wall told its own story. How long? How long does it take? He's thankful in retrospect that he is in this space in time. A hundred and fifty years ago one or both of them would have died. Now he is smiling down at his baby, because he can't keep the gape off his face, protection and relief all painted into an expression of love upon his face. The baby's mother is semi-conscious in a bed in the same room being given a morphine suppository. It will be some hours before she can enjoy the miracle of nature, the grace of God, she – we - have created.

(There Must be an Angel – Eurythmics) 30 877 626

They are in her garden. She has a blanket in the centre of the patch of lawn and lays sunbathing. Her father comes out of the door with a can of lager and lights up a cigarette. The flowers from her mother's funeral lay against the fence behind her, dying.

"I'm only having one!" The Man says defensively to his daughter who, just a few weeks before, lost her mother to alcoholism. She gives out a small chuckle that they both understand. They talk about her mother. Memories she is probably too young to remember. Her voice cracks.

"The last time I saw her, Dad, before she got really ill, I was so horrible to her…"

Her father sighs and shakes his head. "Baby girl, do you think any of that shit mattered to your mother?" He deeply inhales his cigarette and blows out his smoke. "You were her reason for living. Do you think a few harsh words would have made a blind bit of difference to her?" His daughter regains composure because she knows that it is true. They both knew that it was true. A few weeks before her mother got ill her father had seen her at his sister's house and told her that nobody could have loved their daughter any more than she did. She kissed him on the cheek and looked into his eyes and said with more gratefulness than he had ever conceived in his life: "Thank you." He doesn't tell his daughter that the little poem, the words, in the video he made, addressed to his daughter, when her mother passed, had come so easily and effortlessly to him that he felt that they had come from her mother herself.

(The Power of Love – Gabrielle Aplin) 48 371 768

The drug addicts stand on the corner of the estate passing a joint to each other as the young mother approaches pushing a buggy. The passenger an eighteen-month-old boy suckling on a dummy and playing with a wooden toy. The big one, big as in tall, takes a drag of the joint as he spots the young female and hands it to the big one, big as in stocky. He steps out into the middle of the pavement and stands, jail pose. Legs spread apart, both hands down the front of his joggers, back slightly leaning behind – so as to push the penis forward - facing the girl as she joins them. "Hiya, Babe." The girl is stopped in her tracks and the small boy looks up at the man from the toy he is playing with.

"Can I get past, please!?" The young girl says defiantly. She refuses to move onto the road.

"You got a boyfriend, Babe?"

She tuts and moves forward with her buggy almost running it into the leg of the man who has to move quickly to the side. She looks at him with pure hostility as the two of them giggle like hyenas. "Little men!" She spits as she side-eyes them walking past. The tall one moves back into the pavement, resuming the prison pose.

"Small enough to dance on your clit, Babe?"

He does an exaggerated rotation of the hips and again the men laugh like hyenas. He spots an old man across the road shaking his head. He doesn't see the bald eighteen-stone man running along the path behind him. He barely feels the club-hand that snaps his front tooth and nudges the second with the sickening sound of bone uprooted from gum. He doesn't feel it because the contact has knocked him spark out and over the four-foot wall of the garden he was standing by. The big one, as in tall, lays in a garden in the weeds unconsciously spitting out blood from his broken mouth. The other big one, as in stocky, slides along the same wall until there is no wall and falls backwards onto the pavement of the neighbouring street. The man: "That's my daughter yer disrespecting... Cunt!" The girl has stopped. The man across the street is clapping.

"Nice shot, Eddie. Nice shot!"

"Dad! What are you doing? I'm fine."

"Young'un forgot his bottle!"

(Salute – Little Mix) 191 787 209

They spent the whole journey back from the hospital in silence. When they arrived home, he made for the kitchen and poured them both coffees as she headed upstairs. He sat at the breakfast bar for maybe ten minutes before he went looking for her. She was lying in a hot bath, the steam swirling around the room like a sauna, reddening her face but unable to disguise the increased reddening around her eyes. Her pregnant stomach protrudes from the bath water like a maroon-island and her hand is splayed upon it, rubbing it tenderly. He says nothing, strips off his clothes and climbs into the bath behind her. She moves forward a little and says nothing as he places his left arm over her shoulder and across her breastbone. He squeezes her to him as he moves his right arm under hers and onto her hand on maroon-island.

(Forever Song1 – Music by Yakuro) 36

The old man got one of his oldest friends, a Holy man from a righteous family, to conduct the Christening service with him. He had written his own service as opposed to the one practiced by the mainstream clergy of the land; perceived by himself and many like him to be in the pocket of the 'Popish' King, Charles I. Many good religious men had fled, set to the seas in search of a new Jerusalem, in order to escape the autocracy and religious intolerance of the King. He had stayed knowing the back of such intolerance would break and the King would soon be answering to the one true King, Jesus Christ. He passed over his son to his friend and dipped his thumb in the Holy water before tracing it in the shape of a cross on his son's forehead. His friend continued: "I Christen thee," the man stopped as he looked at the name presented to him and looked at the boy's father, who nodded his assent. "I Christen thee Nicholas 'If-Jesus-Christ-had-not-died-for-thee-thou-hadst-been-damned' Barbon."

(Ideal World – The Christians) 1 003 363

Amy Simpson nee Cathcart looked into the sweet blue eyes of her daughter and wondered whether any human was worthy of such a gift from Heaven. The midwife cut the umbilical cord and Carl Simpson dropped onto the bed beside his wife and wiped back her sweat-ridden hair from her face. "She's beautiful, absolutely perfect!" The midwife smiled and left them to it. For a moment in their lives, they would always hold onto. Amy looked down at her daughter with a serene smile: "Jessica! She looks like a Jessica," She looked at her husband. "Gift from God."

(Lifted – The Lighthouse Family) 5 202 586

A couple of days later the Man and his fiancé revisited the hospital. They weren't ready for this, for the possibility of a choice impossible to make. A couple of days previous they had been informed that they may have to make the ultimate sacrifice of termination of one to save the other. They entered the familiar setting of the ultra-sound room, and they watched anxiously as she ran the device around the pregnant woman's stomach. The nurse smiled: "She's back! That's her heartbeat…" The Man wanted to cartwheel around the room and high-five the heartbeat presented on the screen. His fiancé cried with relief. In the doctor's office she explained: "Sometimes the little monkeys grab the umbilical cord so we can't get a reading. We are assuming this was the case with your daughter. You are... 28 weeks in. We need to get to 32. Chances are at 32 we will bring you in and deliver by C-Section."

Four weeks later the twins were born in a special care unit thirty miles away. They were delivered by C-Section and combined, weighed less than four bags of sugar. Next month their son and daughter share their fifteenth birthday.

(Alegria – Cirque De Soleil) 19 977 891

Chapter Nine

Every second, minute, hour, day, year we are getting older and more experienced but are we getting wiser? Smarter? More knowledgeable? More intelligent?

As a machine that processes information that surrounds us it is inevitable – until we choose to deny it, as some do - that that will all depend on the information that is fed to us. I don't just mean media, which is probably far and away the biggest influencer of a sponge-like subconscious, but the views and opinions of those we let into our world and even some we don't. It is difficult to escape this when locked up. A collective consciousness you wanted no part of. I always had a hard time throughout my life because of this. An absorber of mood, it was difficult to pluck myself away from the feelings that surrounded me; to develop the thick skin required sometimes to just survive the day. Soon, I would find out just how thick my skin was, literally.

(Zombie – The Cranberries) 1 121 314 978

He couldn't remember what her position was. She wasn't the Governor, but she was giving a pep talk on what to expect from his stay there. "Try to see it like school."

'Great,' he thought, 'I never liked school!'

She continued. "Oh, and like school, there will be bullies. Just keep your head down, keep yourself to yourself and you should be alright." I was quite good at that, always had been. "And. Stay. Away. From. The. Drugs!"

She pronounced before proceeding to tell of the many wonderful, hygienic, and imaginative ways they were smuggled in and the potential dangers to your health from said transportation. She was particularly adamant in the avoidance of a drug of choice that was hitting the prison called 'Spice.' "It's fish tranquiliser."

He was led with a couple of others to his first home on this misadventure. Keys, locks, red bars, grey and cream walls. It could do with some interior design in here! House Block 4 was the destination of all new prisoners, except sex offenders, and with the others he was ushered into a holding room on the Block. He was speaking to one of the new arrivals, a young fiery kid who he had an immediate rapport with and who was from his neck of the woods, growing up, on the outside. The kid even gave him his teabags which was a bonus because he had opted for the double tobacco 'welcome pack' and so until he was able to secure money and then supplies from the canteen service the prison offered, he was literally a prisoner to those supplies offered him by the prison itself. Eventually he was led to a cell, a double-bunked but unoccupied room. He was thankful for that small arrival mercy. A bed, kettle, cupboard and TV, Sky TV, adorned the room. This is what the outside sees. They have everything they need; they grumble. Yes, if everything you need is a few supplies in your bedroom with the door bolted from the outside and the almost constant sound of banging on walls and hollering. Welcome home to your bedroom in the zoo. First night was a breeze. Cigarettes, tea, and Film 4 before going to sleep.

What you don't realise is that the breeze becomes a wind, and the wind becomes a typhoon and you're right there in the middle of it. Each day is like a single drop of water dropping into the depths of your soul; before you know it, the drops have collected into a pool of stagnant water.

(I Against I – Massive Attack) 700 057

Pi and his family were once again sat by the water. He took his young son to the edge to drink and stood behind as the boy dipped his lips into the shallows of the pool, eyes always on the surface. Always ready, always vigilant, always prepared. His father stood directly behind, his arms apart about a yard, clutching a large rock in either hand. Pi had realised that he no longer had to expend the rocks he now gathered to dissuade the hungry crocs from their assault. The noise from the rocks being smashed together seemed to have the same affect. Perhaps, the crocs had learnt to associate the heavy rocks with attack and therefore looked for easier prey.

(Safe from Harm – Massive Attack) 7 969 535

Epsilon watched Pi and his family. Watched as Pi stood behind his son in a new pose. The Sun was hot and beating down on him as he sat there in the sand away from the comfort of the shade. He sauntered over to where Pi and his son perched at the edge of the pool and made his presence felt. If monkeys could be friends, they could probably consider each other that and they shared eye contact as Epsilon bent down to drink. Pi moved his arms further apart an inch to signify he recognised what was being asked of him. Pi's son finished drinking and moved swiftly towards his mother several feet away behind them. Pi remained in pose as Epsilon continued to drink. He closed his eyes and felt the cold water soothe the furnace of his body. He dipped in his hands in cups and tossed water over his body. The wet hair of his body would offer temporary reprieve for his own family. Once again, he dipped in his face and closed his eyes before hearing the gut-jolting crash of the rocks coming together. The crescendo of noise immediately moved him backwards and away from the water where he saw a lazy pair of eyes appear a couple of meters away from where he had just been. Pi continued to clack the rocks together and the agitated croc, though didn't submerge, did a 180 and began floating away. Pi excitedly smashed the rocks together again as Epsilon watched on and immediately dropped them as a bright orange luminescent light appeared upon their surface and seemed to evaporate in mid-air. Pi and Epsilon looked at each other awestruck, each one seeking acknowledgement from the other of what they had just seen. Pi moved around the rocks tentatively, examining them with his eyes, before moving in closer and touching and quickly removing a finger from the surface of one of the rocks. Epsilon did the same with the other before each of them, rock in hand, headed away to where Pi's family sat fascinated.

(Nimrod – Edward Elgar) 3 657 290

Brian Cathcart, not one to suffer emotion too often or readily, picked up the phone and then put it down, shaking his head. He mulled some more. His pride swelled inside him like over yeasted bread and then the phrase ran in, popped in: 'Some things are bigger than you!' And while the phrase rang in his head, and he repeated it he picked up the handset and dialled the number he had got from the book.

"Adam Cathcart's office please."

The melodic voice of the receptionist replied: "Who shall I say is calling please?"

He thought for a moment and threw the dice of destiny into the air. "It's Brian... His brother Brian."

"One moment please." Now he expected dead air. The click of the phone from the other end. Maybe even some abuse or excuse. Then a voice, low, wary, and sombre: "Hello Brian."

"Hello Adam."

(Brothers in Arms – Dire Straits) 132 566 458

Perhaps the first thought that should pop into your mind as you open up a wrist is: 'What are you doing? What about your children?' Their photographs lay scattered at your feet on the toilet floor. My first thought was: 'Fuck me, that's a lot of blood!' The left arm was always the better blood-giver and the blood from the wound immediately soaked into the left thigh of my jeans. The right wrist took a couple of attempts; lacked the conviction of the first strike. I sat there, in the toilet, in a cell I had minutes before evacuated my cell mate from, claiming a need for peace. "I'll lock it from the outside!" He says as he leaves. Possibly saves my life. Had I locked it would I have opened it up again? Even I don't know the crystal-clear honest answer to that. He hears scurrying outside the door and the excited pitch of voices. They knew, possibly knew in my eyes I was done with this place. The next few minutes are a blur but before I know it one of the guys on the block, who previously had told me where he hid his hooch – a titbit of information I just didn't want to know, was filling the sink with water and told me to submerge my wrists. The block mates from next door walked in and out of the room and offered sympathetic, if slightly disappointed, looks in my direction and on the trail of blood from the toilet to the sink. Healthcare arrives and deals with me. I insist on a cigarette before we leave – it may be the last one I get for a while.

(Streets of Philadelphia – Bruce Springsteen) 148 243 831

Chapter Ten

Sometimes the harsh claws of Fate will place you in positions that throw thoughts, feelings and questions that revolve around in your head like a tumble-dryer. When faced with yourself, are they the harsh claws or tender plucking of maternal fingers?

To imagine that there is a force beyond the material reality we accept can be scary and appear daunting and limiting but could it not just require a slight change in perspective? Is the idea that a force, at times, puts you in such a position that require lessons to be learnt any different from telling a child they cannot go out and play until they have done their homework? We all blame Fate when events are not going our way and yet congratulate ourselves when events turn in our favour. Ironically, it is the greatest of emotions that puts Fate, the Fates, on the highest of pedestals. Not so scary when looked at from that point of view. Free will maybe our own but it doesn't hurt to every now and again have a gentle nudge in a direction by a force that has our best interests at heart; or even a scolding, a lesson to be learnt, when we wander off track, so long as those intentions are for love or doing the right thing or for the purest of intentions. Right? Maybe the narrator is just a dreamer!

(God Moving Over the Face of the Waters Reprise – Moby) 301 889

Saturday Sun strolled high up into the sky and Peter and Nicholas strolled idly down the main parade towards St Martin's Cathedral. The area was alive with the throng of people of all different walks of life; traders, artists, the well-to-do stepping out for an afternoon stroll. Across the street as they continued on, at a table outside one of the taverns, there was a huddle of noisy men around a backgammon board. Already he liked it here. It was a hub of activity with a liberal and cultural diversity all displayed in just one stretch of Utrecht and dressed in a lavish principle of expressional freedom that wasn't afforded in Britain. His eager blue eyes drunk up the scene and he undid the top few buttons to free up his chest and breathe it in. A short distance away there were a huddle of artists all pointing towards the building and sketching and painting away.

"Arteests! Pah!" Peter exclaimed angrily as they approached. Nicholas stopped.

"Why? Why so indignant?"

His Dutch classmate bent down and picked up a handful of dust from the ground and tossed it into the air and the dust dispersed in the soft summer breeze. "Zat is zer artt. Dust in weend. How you say? Temporal?"

"Temporary!"

"Goot. Temporary. Dust gathering dust." Peter grabbed Nicholas by the arm and pointed to where the magnificence of the Cathedral and Tower loomed over them. Nicholas stared down his classmate, who appeared to lose a couple of inches and some of the passion that had stirred within him, immediately removing his arm from his classmate: "Zat is art Neeky! Form, structure, longévité. Zat is art."

Nicholas moved away from his friend and wandered behind the artists watching them work as Peter carried on, flapped a dismissive arm and headed towards the Cathedral. Nicholas sauntered along the line until he stopped behind a young male artist who was mixing a palette and he crouched onto the balls of his heels to admire the sketch the artist had so far constructed. It was good, Nicholas remarked and then furrowed his brows in confusion. In the foreground was an obelisk that appeared to be adorned with hieroglyphics, a structure that had no place in this scene. "Excuse me... Sir." Nicholas raised himself to his feet as the Sun sat on top of the Cathedral roof like a halo. The artist stopped mixing and smiled.

"This monument here?" Nicholas raised a cane, black and silver tipped, towards the canvas then beyond the canvas and to where the structure was supposed to be in the picture. As he pointed his cane the Sun glimmered off the pointed silver end like a small ball of fire. The artist squinted his eyes and said: "Fire-steeck!" Nicholas lowered his cane.

"There is nothing there!" The artist smiled again.

"Engels? Errm English?" The Englishman nodded. "This structure, obelisk, is Flaminio Obelisk at Piazza del Popolo from Egypt. It was erected by Rameses II. No?" Nicholas struggled with the meaning. "Pharaoh of the Exodus... Where else in the World would I be able to paint something so subversive?" Nicholas smiled and offered his hand to the artist who wiped his own with a wet rag.

"Nicholas."

"Jan."

(Black Box – Fantasy) 6 550 207

Brian was sat at a table outside the little café sipping a latte as the Lincoln Continental pulled up. The driver stepped out wearing a suit as immaculate as the car he arrived in. Brian smiled sardonically. Colour co-ordinated, he said silently to himself. The man, a large stripe of grey on either side of his full head of freshly groomed hair, strode over, looking a little agitated.

"Why here Brian?"

"You got old," Brian said smiling as he took a sip of his coffee. "Nice car…" Adam Cathcart looked back in the direction of where he parked and dropped his car keys into his pocket. "An investment. Everyone thinks they're crap so pretty soon they will scrap it and then everyone will want one." Adam took a seat opposite his brother as the waitress popped her head through the door. "Water, in a bottle and an espresso. Thanks." His tone softened this time: "Why here?" Brian put down his cup.

"It was her favourite place to come… And it was where she made me promise I would make amends with you."

"Is that what we're doing? Making amends?" The waitress arrived with Adam's drinks and placed them on the table before him. "Thankyou." The waitress smiled and turned to the other man. "Do you want a refill, Brian?"

"Not just yet." He looked over towards Adam and nodded his head towards him. "This is my brother Audrey." The waitress looked surprised and turned to quickly look at the man she had never seen.

"Oh, I didn't know you had a brother. Oh yes, I see the resemblance. If you need anything else…"

"Adam."

"Adam you just holla… Nice to meet you." Adam smiled and the waitress disappeared back into the café. Adam was about to say something and stopped himself and shook his head instead.

"Her favourite place…" He said, as if to no-one, enigmatically raising his eyebrows and looking away.

Brian sat upright in his chair. "What the fuck is that supposed to mean?"

"Look, Brian, why did you bring me here? You dying or something?" The younger brother slowly sat back in his seat and reached into his inside jacket pocket. He took out a photograph, kissed it and then slid it across the table towards his brother. Adam looked down at it, staring at it long, seeming to hold his breath as if partaking in an underwater challenge, before letting out a deep sigh. He didn't look up from the photograph as he continued: "Ma used to sit right where you are sitting now. I may have been five maybe six. God knows where you were! You used to cry. Cry so much... She couldn't bring you here. She only brought me because I was quiet. Give me something to play with and I was quiet." Adam looked up from the photograph and at his brother. He turned and pointed towards a row of apartment blocks. "You see that apartment block, about 6 down, with the green door?"

"Yeah?"

"That's where 'She' lived, his 'whore!' as she liked to call her." Brian shook his head and was about to argue but Adam continued. "I knew when Dad had arrived there because the cigarettes would come out of her purse. Hands shaking, puffing on it like she had a minute of life left in her. Do you know how hard it is for a boy of that age not to want to go and run to his Dad when he hadn't seen him for weeks, then months?" Adam pushed the photograph of the little girl back across to his brother, bright blue eyes smiling up, blonde curls shimmering in the hospital light, tubes attached to her frail body. Brian swilled off his coffee and stood up.

"Keep the photograph. I know you have no family, but we're all blood!" Brian moved around and behind his brother who sat silently. "She's in St Johns..." He strolled slowly away.

(Max Richter - Never Goodbye) 2 595 570

Whenever I look back at this time, I know the miserable four walls of the place had won, took a major battle in the war that was my life here. I have seen many people since leaving who congratulate my ability to survive for as long as I did. I grimace and usually say something along the lines of: I didn't really actually do that well! "Course you did," they say. I don't show them the small, ugly, horizontal lines across my wrists. "Thanks!" We clink glasses and talk about pool or the England football team or our shit jobs. The dark cloud of that past reality evaporates in the air like broken bubbles. For tonight. Healthcare, I believe, was a blessing and a curse but before any of that even begun, I had to get mended, physically at least. It was the first foray out of this place and the first actual hallucination. I was approximately 4 months in. The doctor, on examining my wounds had obviously given the all-clear to have it professionally stitched. He said something I didn't catch, and I saw Nurse Death do a fist pump to herself. I called her Nurse Death because when she came to my cell, patched me up, I insisted on a cigarette, and she gave me a smile that unnerved me. The dark malt marbles of her eyes unnerve me still and I have no idea what the fist pump was. I have no consciousness of ever seeing her again after this day, so I have no real idea what her position was. The ride to the hospital was strained. The officers were kind, but the small talk diminished when I couldn't even remember where I was brought up, my mind a blur and focused on the outside world I no longer had access to. Trees, grass, roads grey and empty but a welcome sight. People, normal people, just normality roaming, no job to do, no agenda they were subscribing to. Walking through a waiting room full of such people handcuffed to an officer is a lesson in embarrassment I never ever want to experience again. Once is enough, took that medicine thanks, didn't like it.

We moved past them and into a private waiting room and it was sat here, the officers engrossed in magazines, that I had the hallucination that made me feel like I had been submerged in ice water. The room was windowed and so I could see people walk past the room from the waist up and the wife of the victim of my crime walked past the window around the corner and out of sight. I looked at the officers, neither of which had stirred. This was clever and the officers were pro-actors. I was in the middle of some 'programme,' some kind of restorative justice scenario of which everyone was aware but myself. This was a paranoia that would be thematic throughout the next few months. After maybe an hour or so I was moved into an area where a doctor and nurse were going to stitch me up. When I saw that the Doctor and nurse looked like victim and wife, I had an idea I might be fucked. The restorative justice idea stuck to the inside of my mind like a leech, but the rational side of myself tried to grab hold and tell me to be rational. When the nurse dug the needle into the open wound of my wrist, I felt an excruciating pain and looked at her with such indignance she seemed to freeze.

"That REALLY hurt!" I said.

"Sorry!"

Stitched up we made our way back to the place I would call home for the next couple of months and come to realise that the power and weakness of the mind

duel for authority over the vulnerable shell our souls
call home.

(Breathe - Two Steps from Hell) 202 883

Chapter Eleven

Given enough time, applying enough pressure and with all the elemental forces surrounding, a piece of carbon becomes a diamond.

With enough time, pressure and with all the elemental forces surrounding, what becomes of the human mind? Add to that a ravaging curiosity and a quest for one's own Universal truth and something, somewhere, is born within the perceiver. Knowledge is power, they say, but they also say ignorance is bliss. I guess I saw this see-saw within myself and at times would hide under the covers. Shut it out. Let it flow. If you release, where does it go? You don't know, so you hold onto it. A truth I learned within myself was that I wasn't as perfect as at times perceived by others ('You're not Saint Lee!" You hear your wife echo.) because in my wisdom or indeed stupidity I called upon the emotional as well as the actual memory itself. Of everything. Everything! I could ever remember. This was hard. Knowing every time, I did something or lied to someone or about something and painted it off as something else like some bland clay mask upon my face. I had resolved to be honest with myself, not just words said into the wind to placate the maturity and goodness of a Higher Self, but really know myself; the warts and all version, in sickness and in health, not some superficial avatar presented to the world on a grey stage. I wanted the genuine emotion that accompanied the action and when I cried and didn't believe myself, I immediately stopped. 'You're lying to yourself!' If a man was ever able to kick himself, beat himself up, mentally – that is what I was doing most of the time in this 2-month period. Drop a white spot in a heap of black paint and it will make an immediate and visual impact and vice versa. This was me. These days I am a little kinder on myself. I am not in that environment anymore and therefore its impact should have little baring on the now. Obviously, we are shaped and moulded by our experiences. That doesn't mean we cannot break the mould, especially when that mould keeps you in a weakened state of equilibrium.

(Nobody's Perfect – Jessie J) 120 208 883

The watch-maker's son was an eager student of his father's work - to the point of intensity. Whenever his father was at a tricky procedure within the mechanism his son would hover and then pace, his hand across his mouth, almost chewing the skin off his own palm. He had been through many tutors. They couldn't teach him, with his incessant and inane questions. "The answer to the Universe, Robert, begins with a fundamental knowledge of mathematics. Now back to your books." The young boy couldn't understand how this scrawl and that scrawl amounted to a different scrawl. Even when put together in all the complexity and 3D shapes his mind could muster did that shape and that shape come up with that shape! The tutors would shake their heads solemnly at his father: "I'm sorry Jacques… Your son is an imbecile." Sometimes, when watching his father, the young boy would run away and lean against his bed, knees pulled up to his chest by his encircling arms and his head bowed in amongst them. Muttering, incoherent muttering.

(Genius – LSD) 2 284 225

The Man is drinking, he may be a little tipsy and his ex-wife is sat opposite. His daughter, in shorts and a hoodie, sits on a kitchen counter. He is an idiot; he has called for truth moments. An opportunity for any of those present to ask him questions that he promises to answer truthfully. His ex-wife begins: "Why did you leave me?" He doesn't think. Thinking would allow him to find some democratic way to truthfully answer the question.

"You never inspired me." She takes it really quite well. His daughter asks him one: "Why didn't you take your son to golf the other day?" He could lie. He could, because he 'was' called in to work and he went.

"I didn't want to!" And there it is, in the ether! He doesn't realise yet that it will swirl its way back to him. A few days later he goes to see his kids. He talks and talks with his daughter and wonders where his son is. He had had a gig the night before and he would imagine he would be excited to share the experience with his dad.

"Where's ____?"

"He's on the phone to ____ (his girlfriend.)" An hour passes.

"I'll go and see if he's finished on the phone," the Man says nonchalantly, pushing back his chair and standing.

"He's not talking to you," his daughter says.

"Why?" "Because of golf the other day."

"You told him?"

"Yeah. Better that he knows now…" The Man walks through the living room. 'Better he knows now than when? Never.' He feels like saying it, but he doesn't. He knocks and enters his son's bedroom who is laying on his bed, headphones in, gaming.

"How was the gig?"

His son is defiant: "I'm not talking to you!" The Man tickles and tries to cajole his little boy – but the little boy is not 8 years old anymore and he ain't taking no shit. Even from his Ol' Man. His son lectures the Man and all of a sudden, he is himself 8 years old. The man sighs resignedly, "Okay," and leaves his son's room. Back downstairs the Man pretends, not very covertly, that he is okay. Okay with his recent, perhaps rash and intuitively ill-advised, love affair with the unvarnished truth. His daughter looks him in the eyes: "Why are you being so passive-aggressive?"

"What does that actually mean – passive-aggressive?" Her father retorts sulkily. He shrugs his shoulders, and they smile at each other. It is conflict, but they love each other immensely, so it is actually a discussion. The father knows his children are growing up fast and respects that, but Dad becoming a little terser and more combative is a consequence of that.

"When I was a kid there was no passive-aggressive… Just passive or aggressive! You want me to be honest?

I'm neither passive nor aggressive. I'm pissed off because my son won't talk to me!" They talk some more
and as they do his son enters the kitchen and sits on the
kitchen worktop.

"You want to know how my gig went?"

"Of course."

"I've got some photographs on my phone."

The Man walks over to his son: "Let's have a look
then." He scrolls through. "Did you not freeze at all?"
The boy nonchalantly replies no, like the question is
even strange. He places his phone on the table for his
family audience.

"This is the set we did." He presses play and the music rings out as he nervously moves into the living room
anxiously perched on the arm of the sofa chair as his
immediates listen. "See this bit coming up now Dad,"
he interjects. "This is the bit you said needed more
power." It plays. "Has it got more power?"

The father nods smiling. "Yes, son, it has!"

Order is restored in Familytopia.

(Family Affair – Mary J Blige) 282 056 294

"I won't do it! I won't! I won't! I won't!" The King
slams a red velvet-gloved hand on the thick oak table
before him. His goblet wobbles but does not fall.

"Sire I implore you to reconsider. France will be on our shores this very year, this very week, maybe, if you do not curtail this threat within our midst." The King takes a long gulp of his drink and looks at his Advisor over the brim of his receptacle with contempt. "Of course, the choice is yours, My Lord, I am only here to Advise." The King puts down his cup with a slow and careful deliberation. A conscious show of control. Control of something if only his own drinking vessel.

"Leave me." The Advisor gets to his feet and heads for the door. "I've dealt with snakes all of my life!" The King shouts. "ALL OF MY LIFE!"

(It's My Life – Talk Talk) 15 348 572

Brian Cathcart was brewing tea when he heard the screech of tyres outside his house. He moves to the window to investigate and spots the car parked carelessly in his drive before he hears the heavy banging on the door. He picks up his tea and answers.

"You have no right!" The man says barging past him and into the living area.

"Come in!" Brian remarks following. "Tea?"

"No, I don't want fucking tea." Adam paces the room agitated. "You call me and sit there all sanctimonious like you were the only one who give a damn!" Brian sits as his brother spits fireballs at him. He'll take the fireballs for her. Adam plucks at his jacket and his pants. "This, this," he gestures towards his car outside then raises his arms in a circular motion. "Fuck, all of it... All of it! Was to just impress her. Get one fucking warm word out of the woman. It never came, Brian, it never came!" Adam drops heavily into a chair opposite his brother and puts a hand across his eyes.

"Scotch?" Brian says softly.

"Yeah!" Adam replies wiping his eyes.

(Hurt – Johnny Cash) 124 849 290

Chapter Twelve

If your mind is telling you one thing, but every other sense in your body is telling you it's not real, how do you actually distinguish what is real and what is illusion?

Boots are flaking, laces are disintegrating, you tiredly flip off the footwear which somersaults across the bedroom. You look down to spot a big toe poking from a hole in your sock; the nail, black, broken and jagged wiggles as if saying hello. Socks come off and lie in the middle of the room like cheese and bacon puffs. You let out a sigh and recline back on the bed, asleep in seconds. Today was tough. Tomorrow will probably be better. Everything is better after a nap, something to eat, a shower. Tomorrow the hard balls of your feet will chart the same course; feel the same hard floor beneath your feet. The ragged sleeves of your jumper will get more ragged, the jeans muckier then more faded. You will feel the same hard corners of things, feel the same stresses, encounter a similar fatigue. The average person thinks that the dreamer, the illusion seeker, the fantasist - if you like - lives in a perpetual state of fantasy. Like Unicorn horns are poking from behind every tree, fairies dancing and playing mischievously among the daffodils. It is seldom the case. The artist that draws on fantasy, that takes the surrealist often unique way of looking at things and converts it into art is more often than not a prodigious sketcher, drawer, painter of the real. Of the world laid out in front of them like a stage show. Looking at things from a different perspective generally means they have already seen it from the majority view. The populist view. The dreamer, the fantasist, is actually a tireless student of reality. The tireless student of life becomes a willing participant in a depth beyond the reality they can actually see.

(Both Sides Now – Joni Mitchell) 2 574 400

In Healthcare it got silly. So, so many coincidences it was difficult to discount it as such. Several weeks before, his cellmate, the same one he had shooed from the room when he cut his wrists, told him: "Stop! Stop connecting the dots!" He can't remember the exact circumstance of such a warning but knew he must have been in some upper echelon state of anxiety. The dots just kept coming – and he kept joining them. He couldn't help it; it was his mind. Now, in healthcare, the dots ran riot and the fiery electric strings that branched from his neurons connected this dot to that dot until they were lit up like a big City on Google maps. The subject matter of the TV ceased to be a product of storytelling fiction but a loosely based narrative of his life and circumstance. Songs on the radio, same. They say that we only concentrate on the relevant parts of a Horoscope and discount the rest. He was focusing on the relevant with the attuned skill and concentration of a professional darts player. How much did he actually discount? Every so often he would hear relatives calling his name from the TV as a background to whatever it was, he was watching. Had the mind hatched a plan? Entertain yourself or die in the empty bleakness of this room? The TV become a focal point and a significant component in his conspiracy theories. Somehow it was absorbing him, absorbed him all along, knew his weaknesses, knew everything about him and spat those back out into his brain – sometimes into the brains of others. Sometimes it helped. Sometimes he would ask an Officer to remove it from his room. Sometimes it would end up sailing through the air to the nearest concrete caress. Certain people had access to this information, including certain prisoners, but it was a two-way street - he could hear them too. Ants would figure strongly in his thoughts in the first few weeks for reasons he will go into later, but he believed he had picked up some kind of antennae. He called himself Ant Man. It was only after he left 2 years later that he realised a film of the same name had been released a month or so previous to this bizarre episode of his life.

(Solitaire – The Carpenters) 133 116

Robert was re-arranging the timepieces in his father's workshop. "Father is working on you tomorrow…" He moved one of the metal objects behind another and delicately placed it down. "Don't you worry, my friend, not to worry, Father will fix you up good and proper, shiny and new!" Jacques worried about his son. He was worrying deeper by the day and shook his head as he stood watching Robert from the doorway behind him. He moved silently away and wrapped a cover around himself and laid upon his bed and pulled his legs into his chest and thought of his wife. I miss you, he said to himself, I miss you so much!

(Father and Son – Cat Stevens) 19 397 517

Many years later the Man got each of them together and he asked the question that had dogged him, especially after his years away. "What happened that night? You remember it?" His best friend nodded his remembrance of it. His best friend was home from Germany, where he now lived, shared a life with his wife and the children none of his circle ever thought he would entertain. Now he was Mother, his wife a bigwig in some company and now the main bread winner. He received the text of his impending arrival and knew that as ever it would cause conflict, a wave upon the calm waters of his marital life. His wife and his best friend had never really seen eye to eye and didn't still so many years on.

"You drop everything for him!" His wife would say and he would listen to the rant 'blah, blah' knowing he was going to go anyway with or without her approval. She was going away for the weekend anyway so what fucking difference did it make!? He tries to pacify so that she doesn't hit him with the oars of his simple little wooden boat floating along on serene seas. He is being unfair, he is being unfair still, painting a dynamic that is as illusional to him now as it has always been to the impartial observer. Even the not so impartial observer. His soft personality had always been perceived as the weak partner. It wasn't the case; it had never been the case. People mistake laissez faire for the henpecked husband or the manipulated friend. He thinks his best friend believes such because it is such a grind for him to get out and play. "I bet she controls the remote in that household," he imagines people are saying, his friend included, forgetting the fact that when he lived with him, it was himself who sought control of the remote. "Do you know what?" The man cries: "I never fucking needed the remote! It didn't in the slightest bit interest me. I have books, whims, hobbies, a whole castle full of activities within my head that don't require the choice of whatever mass media production you want to feed on!" And there it is. Laissez faire attitude to life, to the remote, to the rant he will receive because neither one was grown up enough for him to accept either one's place in his life. He loves them both and that is that. The dynamics will have to work, straighten themselves out, because he is uncompromising. They arrange to meet at his brother's flat, which, in actual fact is his best friends flat which he rents to his brother. The drinking commences, another old friend is there, and they reminisce about the time the four of them went to Amsterdam together. Incidentally, it is on this trip that his best friend met his prospective German wife. Conversation flows as easily as the drink. Words, memories, and laughter hang in the air like the thick cannabis smoke that swirls about the room. The man doesn't do cannabis, never really did – he's paranoid enough. They agree to take their sociability to the local pubs and swill off their drinks eagerly and the troupe march off, set sail for the high seas. In the first pub, it is busy, but one of the group spot the Man's ex-fiancé sat in there with her boyfriend. He's met her boyfriend a few times, at gatherings at parties, there is not a single shred of animosity between them. That relationship ended long, long ago. They have a daughter together and they care about one another and that is that. There are no complications, no residual resentments, just simplicity. A simplicity imbued within the marrow of the Man and perhaps his ex-partner too. The other boys make their introductions and our group head outside into the beer garden. She joins us outside. She knows everybody present and we talk. We are discussing Brexit, differing views, heated discussion, particularly among the brothers. One of them is now, in fact, a Brit and a European. The other brother thinks that Britain is under the control of an autocratic European elite, some sinister Volturi-like organisation. It is all very serious and all very light-hearted too. The Man and the other friend share a look of amusement and giggle into their beers. A little later, the Man, his best-friend and his ex-partner are stood near the bar talking about their times in Coventry. They all lived together for a time in a dinghy little house, on a street with overgrown hedgerows, not far from the canal. He asks the question: "What actually happened that night?" They both know which night he is talking about.

(Memories – Maroon 5) 764 044 782

Nicholas and Jan agreed to meet the following day. Same place, outside the Cathedral. He saunters out of his university apartment, across the square and along the parade towards his destination. He is never hurried, never rushed, as controlled as the measured beating of his heart. There are no tradesmen around today, it is Sunday, and he is in the epicentre of flourishing Religion. Tolerant, but Religious. Malleable, but righteous. The artists are out again, and he spots a young girl, maybe a year or two younger than himself, sat at a table outside a tavern sketching the colourful rows of houses opposite herself. Nicholas gravitates towards her, unaware of how far off a straight line he has veered to make her acquaintance. The girl looks up, unperturbed, and then carries on drawing. "May I?" The young Englishman points his cane at her sketchbook. She nods her assent and turns the picture towards him, and he nods with approval. "It's good. You have a real talent... Do you mind if I sit a while?" The girl seems to somersault over her words.

"Thank you and no, please." She offers him a seat.

"I'm Nicholas."

"Arabella." She puts down her sketch on the table and turns to face the man, the stranger, the invader of her creative peace. "You must be at the University, no?"

"That obvious?"

"With all due respect, sir, you don't look very much like a native!" They talk about university life, about his life back home, about her aspirations to become an artist, to follow in the footsteps of Leyster and how she admired the works of van de Passe and the works and ideology of Anna Maria van Schurman. She talked with such colour and passion that time flowed by like a fast-flowing stream. Nicholas looked towards the Cathedral in the distance. "I'm sorry," she said, a little embarrassed. "You need to be somewhere? Meeting?" Nicholas smiled back at her, her waxen complexion looking a little flushed, blushed.

"Nothing that can't wait. I'm sure Jan will still be there. He has a painting to finish."

"This Jan? An artist?"

"Yes."

"Then you must go! Artists can be…" She pulled a series of faces that made Nicholas laugh loudly.

"Crazy?"

"Yah… crazy!" She giggled with him. Nicholas raised himself up and straightened his coat. "It has been a pleasure, Arabella, I hope we will cross ways again soon."

"I am out here, somewhere, drawing every Sunday." Nicholas moved away, heading for the Cathedral, before turning: "By the way," he said pointing his cane towards her. "Those are an extraordinary pair of earrings." Once again Arabella smiled, embarrassed.

"Alas, they are not real pearls, Nicholas, not real."

"Never the matter," he said turning around. "They are beautiful all the same!"

(All the Time in the World – Louis Armstrong) 3 361 329

Chapter Thirteen

We indulge in escapism hoping it will all fade away. The monster slithering with serpentine proficiency through the waters; snake like body, rolling and moving with indifference but with menace above the calm lake. So, we look away, move our feet out of the water and will the monster to the bottom of the murky depths.

The monster leaves and so do we. Some, with an assurance, a personal promise, that they will return fully armoured, sword in hand and take the head of the creature that incapacitates them. We all come back, we have no choice really, but if we stay on the riverbank long enough maybe we can chart its movements, spot its weaknesses, find an opening. The monster confronted, even just viewed in all its scariness, begins to lose some of the charm of its horrific aesthetic. Stay a while, watch as the vividness of its colour fades and the dangerous coils rolling in and out of the lightening shade of waters become thinner. If we remain long enough armed with enough faith, love and support perhaps the Sea-Monster becomes just a big Pike. Capable of biting but not half as deadly as you first thought. Some will feed the fat belly of the monster with an apathetic indifference to the destructive quality of their nature – a non-consequentiality. Some will run. Take another drink, pop another pill, cook up another illusion – an illusion where the monsters are not so scary.

(Storm – Vanessa Mae) 12 779 914

They are talking about what the counsellor said to her: "They think it has something to do with my Mum…" The Man looks at her and offers his own take and the first and most honest thing that came into his mind: "I never ever really got that impression!"

"Thaaaank Youuuu!" She pronounces excitedly leaning forward. "It has nothing to do with Mum."

"So, what is it then?" He asks.

She shrugs her shoulders. "I don't know… Just addiction innit?"

The Man is thinking and exhales his cigarette. "Do you know what I think it is?" He leans forward. "I think you think you are indestructible!"

She neither endorses nor disagrees. Of course, she is not indestructible, and apathy and indifference colonised her spirit. Sometime later he is stood on one side of a hospital bed looking down at her yellow frail body and holding her hand, she doesn't seem to know who he is. He doesn't think he sees fear, just oblivion in her wandering eyes. The fears are streaming down the sides of his daughter's face sitting and talking to her Mum on the other side of the bed. He'd already spoken to a nurse before going in: "I'm sorry, her liver is too far gone, beyond repair. I'm sorry."

She isn't leaving this room. His daughter's phone rings, and it is her Grandad on Facetime. She answers and holds the phone up to her Mum. He talks to his daughter and the Man wants to be anywhere, anywhere in the world but here at this moment and looks away from the scene as his eyes become rain spattered windows.

(Viva Forever – The Spice Girls) 459 885

The big one, as in tall, reclines on his mattress, leaned against his bedroom wall so that his head and chest are at a ninety-degree angle. He doesn't feel the discomfort. He is fucked. His girlfriend is in the same room sat in front of a portable full-length mirror applying the lipstick she stole from Primark. She looks in the mirror at her fella and tuts before returning to her self-care routine. She doesn't mind staggering around town, unkempt hair dripping down under her baseball cap, asking for change with rolling eyes in a state of oblivious bliss, but she won't leave the house without her lipstick on. A mantra she will live and die by: "I NEVER leave the house without ma lippy on... Never!" She is applying when she hears the thundering on the door. Her hand jumps and applies the lipstick to her nose.

"Shit!" She pulls out a baby wipe and jumps to her feet and looks with panic at her boyfriend who has just miraculously re-emerged from his deep brown sleep. The door bangs again. This time it sounds like a foot knock. The big one, as in tall, and his girlfriend are signalling frantically between themselves. He has just communicated that he is dead if the knocker gets in using the miracle of hands and eye gesture. She hurries to the window and pulls back the cream net curtains, they were white, and opens the window out onto the street where a large built man in Burberry cap is looking up in fury: "Open the fuckin door Tanya or I'm gonna fuckin kick it in!"

"He's not here Sully I swear!" "Don't fuckin lie to me yer rat!"

"I'm not, swear on our Reece's life, I'm not!"

"Where's he?"

"At his Mams Sully. I think she's gonna do him a borrow!" The man's pose changes from white hot fury to cold menace. He points at the girl: "Tell him... You listening, Tanya?"

"Yeah, yeah." She affirms nodding frantically.

"Tell him he best have it tomorrow or I'm gonna break his fuckin legs... Right?" She nods. He shouts louder. "Tomorrow Sid! You hear me, ya rat?"

"He's not here Sully, I swear..."

"Whatever!"

The big one, as in stocky, walks off down the street fists clenched. His school reports had always said he never applied himself or got in with the wrong crowd. They were right about the latter but wrong about the former. With the right motivation Sid could apply himself better than anyone in town. The teachers would be proud. Watch how he manoeuvres round his vicinity avoiding everyone he owed money too while earning a lucrative shoplifting living. He was a gutter grafter, a pavement entrepreneur, a self-interested piece of shit but 24 hours later the big one, as in tall, is sniffing coke off his living room table with Tanya, lippy decoratively applied, and the other big one, big as in stocky. Empty cans of Carling dot the floor and the men have their arms over each other's shoulder chatting shit about respect. Today life is good in Drugtopia.

(Perfect Day – Lou Reed) 79 279 600

"What actually happened that night?" We'd had it plenty of times in our youth, my best friend and me. We always used to stay at mine listening to tunes from a club popular in town at the time called The Havana. On one particular occasion we experimented with the notion that we were telepathic when under its influence. We were right… Or maybe we weren't. The problem with drugs is it can addle your reality or remembrance of things. Fact is, he asked me at least three obscurities of thought that I nailed. His proof to me that I had been correct - an arm full of goosebumps. We have talked about it since. He is so much more logical than me and said something along the lines of how many did you get wrong? He is right. We were off our tits and could have been playing this game for hours. Problem is, I have no recollection of any that I got wrong. In Coventry we decided, now in our early twenties and not in our early teens, that we would try it again. The drug, not the telepathy. My girlfriend at the time and not so long after the mother of my eldest child secured the merchandise. It was her city after all. Red Dragon the acid was called and we all took one each. We are playing monopoly my best friend and I. Girlfriend is on the sofa in her own world. The music is playing. The loud sound of the monopoly money being shuffled in my friend's hand overtakes every other sound and I look at him and he looks at me and we both know we are about to lose it. It is late in the game, it must be, because my properties have houses on them and it is at this moment looking, looming, over my properties that I have a feeling so intense it takes me out of my head. I literally lost all consciousness without becoming unconscious. I have lost memories of a night on several occasions but never have I had a feeling that my conscious mind was snatched from me. It returned, seconds? Minutes later? My friend and I are stood out in the garden, and I am looking around myself as if waking from a sleepwalk and he is exhaling loudly, thumb and forefinger moving up his forehead up to his hairline, "What the fuck just happened? What the fuck just happened there?" I can't answer. I was hoping he could, or my girlfriend could. They offer a story, many years later, about how she had got into the bath fully clothed with no water in for no apparent reason and we had started laughing before I got some jealous insecurity and ended up outside. I don't believe it; it doesn't ring true in my core or exist as a memory within me. For the rest of the night me and my girlfriend sit huddled together on the sofa each escaping a bad trip. I am climbing down from the top of a large sparkling tree for hours until the drug wears off. We never take it again.

(White Rabbit – Jefferson Airplane) 63 690 925

Nicholas reached Jan among a semi-circle of onlookers. He decided to join the group rather than disturb the frantic artist putting his finishing touches to his days' work, his creative participation as he would call it. The general consensus among the whispering eyes were that they were in the company of a great artist, but if he knew it, Jan didn't acknowledge it, at the time. Now he was done and turned the painting over to scrawl his initials on the back with a thick pencil. JvdHeyden. The onlookers peered closer to read the scrawl. Very clever, Nicholas thought, very clever indeed. The painting was as yet unfinished, perhaps the rest would be applied in some studio, so this would probably be the last time the artist would get an audience for this particular work. The captive audience now had a name to attach to the art. The artist now had a name that could be sought. He had just marketed his wares within a sphere of art. A black-bodied mass was leaving the Cathedral as Jan began packing away. A middle-aged man approached and offered his hand to Jan: "Great work, young sir, great work!"

Jan shook it gratefully and seeing Nicholas amongst the onlookers gave an almost imperceptible nod. Nicholas recognised this was the showmanship of the artist. The hard/soft sell. An artist could be a prune most of the time if they wanted and put it down to artistic temperament, but there comes a time when they want to endear, and this was Jan's time. More people offered their hands and congratulations before dispersing and leaving the artist to roll up his work and place it in a tube which he wore upon his body like a quiver. The two men shook hands: "Hello Nicholas, I thought you were not going to come…"

"A beautiful distraction… Great work, Jan." He said, with a depth in the words that meant more than the art itself. Jan caught on.

"Ah, selling ourselves is part of the process Nicholas. Just a part of the artistic process. Whatever beliefs, however detached they want to be from society sometimes, they still need to eat!" The artist tapped Nicholas' back. "Let us walk." They turned and headed slowly up the main strip. "A beautiful distraction you say?" Nicholas smiled but kept his face forward. "Ah, a girl? Ya?" Nicholas looked at him and nodded. "Dutch?"

"Yes…" Quietly. "Yes." Jan stopped.

"Be careful there, Englishman…" Jan warned and turned to face the confused Englishman. "Umm, this whole country is going through a change… Erm an evolution…" He rolled his hand. "And none more so than its young ladies. You ever see swans fly, my friend?" Nicholas shook his head. "That is the Dutch girl Nicholas… Swans that fly!" Nicholas walked on, quicker, frostily faced.

"It was just a conversation!" Jan caught up to Nicholas, placed his hand on his back and tapped it with affection and the two strolled again. Jan led them down a side street, into a building, up some wooden steps and into a single room where his art adorned the shabby walls like jewels in tin clasps. He swept some items with his hand off a small table and bid Nicholas to sit down, but he chose to remain standing, admiring the gallery. Jan dropped onto a small bed, his only amenity in the tiny room.

"Your art is superb!" Nicholas said moving along the wall taking in the scene of each picture before sitting and facing Jan. Jan sat fully on his bed and pulled up his knees to his chest. "That is not the real art, Nicholas, not by a long way. That is conjecture, a view, an interpretation…" Nicholas placed his cane on the floor.

"You talk in riddles, Jan, swans, not art…"

"Your friend is a fool, Nicholas. From yesterday, your friend, but he is right about one thing… Art is dust in wind. It is a moment in time. Sometimes, I begin a work and it changes many times from that first moment to this." He gestured to his walls. "The work will remain. True. But the artist changes, that is the real art! We are art, each and every one of us, in what we say in what we do. That is the real influence. A few brushstrokes on a canvas, a beautiful Cathedral, a waterfall, a sunset. That is merely an image, an artistic impression. How it makes us feel, what it makes us do, that is real art. That is the art that can change things. That is art that can change the world. If only our own."

"It is still art!"

"Depends on your perception of art, my friend. You see art as a finished article. A full stop? Look again at my wall Nicholas, at the pictures…" Nicholas obeyed and scanned the wall. "That one there… Does it make you want to submerge in the cool blue waters of the lake? Feel the fish brush across your body as you swim in it? Ah, I see by your reaction that the thought never crossed your mind. What does it make you feel, what does it make you think?"

"It makes me curious about such a beautiful place…"

"Then my part in creative participation is in the right direction. That girl? The girl today, how did she make you think and feel?" Nicholas stood and shook his head at Jan who sat smiling up at him.

"I tell you what your art does make me think… You shouldn't be living in a hovel like this!" He gestured to the room.

"Aah, temporary lodgings, my friend, I leave in 6 days."

"You're leaving?" Nicholas asked disappointed. Jan got up off the bed.

"Let us get a drink my friend. One thing about Dutch men I forgot to mention, Nicholas, they follow the swans. Follow the swans." Nicholas reached the door before turning around.

"I wanted to buy her some pearl earrings." Jan banged his hand on the bed excitedly, laughing.

"Then do it my English friend! Do it!" He put his arm around Nicholas' shoulder, and they headed out of the room.

(Swan Lake – Tchaikovsky) 5 562 532

Chapter Fourteen

Everybody is looking outside of themselves for a hero, somebody to look up to. Everybody is looking for someone else to provide them with the answers. Maybe, just maybe.

There are many rocks in the way, unforgiving gnarly thorn bushes hanging over the sides of the path we sometimes walk. What are we to do? Do we see the obstacles, sense the danger of that way forward and turn around, leaving the unchartered land of our lives and future still unchartered? We get knocked down every day. It shouldn't be the knocking down that should affect us, affect us to our core, it should be our reaction to such events. How can the little things affect us so when we are a species who, from an early age, know that we are here to serve such a short time in the scale of things? We are a species who have the conscious awareness that we are born to die and yet we accept this with an apathetic but strong acceptance that should make some of the follies of our daily existence fade into the obscurity they deserve. Maybe when we cherish life, the rollercoaster of existence we all ride, appreciate the people we love and those that have taught us some of our harshest lessons, that we can embrace our inevitable expiration with a courageousness, dignity and fearlessness the soul deserves.

(Hero – Mariah Carey) 295 924 412

The young Boy is walking through the big city streets of London with his grandad, the hero of this young boy's narrative. They are there for a few days because his grandad is taking his grandson, his blue-eyed boy, to see the Trooping of the Colour, tickets he secured from a good friend he knew in the Coldstream Guards. London is magnificent. The Boy loves it; the hectic pace; the Bohemia of Camden; the riches of Bond and Oxford Street. Ordinarily the boy hates to walk, dawdles, he was continually harangued about such a thing, but here there is no dawdling. Walking in wide-eyed wonder at all the sights. They take a river trip down the Thames and as they go under Tower Bridge the drawbridge slowly rises. His grandad tells the Boy that in all the multitude of times he has been to London he has never seen the drawbridge rise and the boy glows with a sense of glorious entitlement. The Man knows that the drawbridge rises quite often – because he just wiki'd it – but the Boy didn't! On the day of the main event, they charter a course through London on foot, dressed in their finest, if only modest attire. Suited and booted. As they got closer to Buckingham Palace, the throng the pair travelled in, walking side by side, became better dressed. The hire cars and open-topped buses replaced by shimmering blue Jags and sparkling black Rollers. The novelty hat and T-shirted tourist replaced by the immaculate grey and dark suited strangers all heading for the same destination. It was like the hurry up for the luxury buffet marquis at Ascot races. The champagne set. London's finest all congregating on the location of the Queen's formal birthday celebration. They had a good spot directly opposite the Palace and the Boy watched with fascination. His grandad pointed out the Prime Minister at the time, Margaret Thatcher, some couple of hundred yards away in a crowd to the right. He has no idea that his working-class hero is pointing out the woman considered by many to be the scourge of the working class. The Boy doesn't remember his grandad ever saying such a thing or anything of the political landscape and the Boy never really cared nor cares still. The Boy has an innocence of such things the Man has carried with himself into adulthood. Perhaps the Boy felt as the Man does now that change is not necessarily with the bloodied and battered fists of Revolution but with an Evolution in the softly beating heart of swansong. The Queen looked every inch the monarch, inspecting the parade, watching, scrutinizing from horseback, the last year she would attend her own service in this manner. London had been magnificent, a real eye-opener for the young Boy, but he remembered an overheard conversation his grandad had with his Coldstream Guard friend which the Boy didn't understand at the time. It was along the lines of: "I love London, I love being in London, but I hate the fact that some of the people were looking at me like I was some kind of nonce because I was with our Lee!" I didn't understand what that meant as a kid. Did it deter the Old Man? He took me the following year to see the Trooping again. I saw the Fat Boys, an American rap band dancing and messing about outside the gates of Buckingham Palace, I told my grandad, but he had no idea who they were. That year the Queen inspected her troops from a carriage. Her trusty, faithful mare had retired.

(A String of Pearls – Glenn Miller) 1 273 817

Adam drove past several times before he finally stopped outside of the hospital. He'd even pulled into a fast-food restaurant at one point and ate there for the first time in several years, since college even. Sucking up the cold sweetness of a strawberry milkshake, Adam Cathcart decided he had to see her, even if it was to confirm his own reasoning that any kind of attachment was a foreign, alien land to him now. Now he sat outside the hospital in his run around about to engage - or maybe not - when he saw the stocky huddled figure of his brother entering the hospital, head down. Should he wait? He let out a deep sigh, flicked on the radio – Islands in the stream that is what we are – flowed melodiously from the speakers and Adam reclined his seat, and thought of Rosa, and waited.

(Islands in the Stream – Dolly Parton & Kenny Rogers)
25 693 055

Brian entered the room to two blue jewels gleaming at him. Her Mother looked lazily from the magazine she was browsing and dropped it to the floor.

"Grandad!" The girl vaulted off the bed and into the arms of her grandad. He held her tightly and then stroked back her blonde curls.

"How are you, Princess?" He said kissing her forehead.

"I feel good… Do you want to see my pictures?" He put her down.

"Hell yeah!" He said enthusiastically and she hurried to her bedside cabinet to gather up her art. He moved over to his daughter who smiled up at him. He kissed the top of her head. "You look tired, Sweetheart. You need some sleep."

"I'm okay," she said. "I'm so glad you came." And she looked over to her excited daughter and started crying.

"Mommy! What's wrong?" The girl plucked a picture from the pile and gave it to her mom: "Here, you like this one… This one will make you happy." Amy Simpson laughed through her tears.

"Thank you, Angel." Brian scooped up his granddaughter and moved to a chair by the window.

"Let's see then Picasso…"

For an hour Brian Cathcart flicked through the pages of his granddaughter's artistic interpretations offering his own inimitable explanation of their excellence and where if any they could be improved. She sat on his lap, and they were both lit up like alien Suns.

"Shall we go get some lunch?"

"Yeah!" She jumped down. He looked at his daughter: "Is that okay? She allowed to leave the ward?" Amy Simpson stood and picked up her bag. "It's going to have to be, isn't it! Should be okay if she pops something on over her nightie. Grab your cardy, Honeysuckle." They headed for the entrance of the room.

"What you going to get Grandad?"

"Imma gonna get me some macaroni," he said in his worst Italian accent.

"Imma gonna get me some ice cream!" Jessica copied, taking her grandad's hand and they headed for the cafeteria.

(Can You Feel the Love Tonight – Elton John) 30 859 718

Toby sat on the top of a hill way out of sight of the divisions on the field below him. Banners of war rippled slightly in the light summer breeze. The young boy watched with interest as skirmishes broke out in various areas of the arena before him. Now he focused his attention on the man who just a few of hours before had sought him out in the woods near his home. He was pacing backwards and forwards agitatedly on a fine black horse; he appeared to be addressing the troops before him. On the opposing side of the battle a Captain sat at the back of his army flanked on either side by a line of shining knights. He sat motionless and cool on his white horse. The other, the man who had introduced himself as knowing the boy, looked angry and upset, noticeably jolted by the way in which the conflict had been unfolding. He wheeled his horse around to face the enemy as his cavalry moved through the ranks to join up with him. He kicked his horse into action and the canter soon turned into a charge and he kicked his legs violently at the beast who responded in kind with more speed, so much so that he was yards and then metres in front of his own cavalry. He appeared to be charging straight for the white-horsed captain who remained motionless throughout and with his black horse flying like an express train, he quickly lowered a light lance which seemed to break in the breastplate of an advancing knight. The unfortunate knight seemed to sit still, unharmed for just a second, before slithering gracelessly from his mount and helmet down to the ground. The angry combatant drew out his sword and pointed it to the man on the white horse, who remained motionless still, as a line of infantrymen moved rapidly in front of him, their weapons, their pikes, tilted upwards from their kneeling bodies like piranha's teeth, awaiting the mad cavalryman. Archers from the left were pulling back their bows, but Toby noticed that one of the knights' broke ranks from the line and moved forward on his horse shouting something at the archers who immediately stood down. The knight returned to his position. Toby had seen battle before. His father had been a prominent captain in the forces of the Duke of Gloucester, but he was dead, killed in battle. He hadn't seen it, but his mother had received a letter from the King personally with a message of her husband's demise. She had told the boy that his father had died with honour fighting side by side with the duke. The duke was now King. When the pikemen pierced the breast of the black charging horse that tried to vault the line and the angry man was flung over the horde of men Toby saw the gold circle fall from the man's head and realised that the man he was watching, the man he had spoken to, was indeed the King. The King rose off a knee and gathered up his crown as the pikemen surrounded him and the Standard Bearer of his enemy rushed him using the sharp point of the banner in lance-like fashion, missed, and was dealt a hacking blow to the back by the surrounded King. The horseman floundered in his saddle as the King fought on. He slayed and slayed until a knight, and then another, and another, galloped in a procession towards the horseless King and sliced at him as pike went into distracted boar under the armpit. The King would not drop. Again, the knights rode past hacking at the floundering man who still appeared to be shouting at the captain on the white horse who remained motionless. Two of the knights jumped from their horses and double sworded the King before one of them removed the circle from his head and rode over to the captain and presented it on his head. The remaining knights slashed at the prostate body of the fallen King, the angry cavalryman, the man who knew Toby. He watched and remembered the man's words: "Should I fall… Never, ever expose yourself to anyone. That you knew me, that I was ever here in your presence."

The boy had nodded perplexed. Now he moved from the hill and back through the woods towards home. This event would haunt his dreams for months.

(Contempt – George Delerue) 135 102

Adam watched as Brian crossed the road behind him and disappeared into the distance, head hunched, shoulders stooping. He flicked off the radio, put on a baseball cap and headed into the hospital. After a few enquiries he was outside her room. Door closed; he looked through the glass window. The bed was made, some papers were neatly stacked on the bedside cabinet, the only evidence that anyone had actually ever occupied this room. Where were they? Had she moved to another ward? Was he too late? He stepped backwards, eyes on the door and dropped onto a chair. A mural painted on the inside of the walls of the ward had a Sun shining brightly in a clear azure sky, laughing children with lollipops and ice creams as big as their joyful heads made up the foreground as a carousel appeared to be turning behind them. The horses of the carousel were magnificent white and brown and black unicorns. A large silver Moon adorned the other side in a perfect opium-black background. The same laughing smiling children were looking up, gaping at the bright splash of fireworks that lit up the black sky of this part of the mural. Joy and wonder. What it is to be a child! What it is to be a child, Adam thought and dropped his head in his hands and squeezed his eyes together. "Are you okay, Mr Mister?" Adam looked up to see a young girl with eyes like blue diamonds stood before him. A pink scarf wrapped around her head.

"I'm good thank you, young lady… And I'm Adam."

"Like the first man?" Adam was taken aback, and his brows furrowed.

"Yes, like the first man."

"And the first sinner!?" Adam choked a little, laughing.

"Yes, that too! I suspect he wasn't the last!" The girl laughed. "You are a remarkably intelligent young lady."

"Thank you. Mr Adam. My Mommy said that as a penance Adam would create the human race and it would be our job to make it up to God for the sins of our first father…"

"And Eve?" Adam asked testing. The girl put her finger to her lip in concentration.

"And Eve too!" She said nodding her head. "But you are not called Eve… Do you know anyone called Eve?"

"No," Adam replied chuckling. "But if I ever come across one, I'll make sure to point out her responsibilities. What is your name, Young Lady?"

"Jessica… My Mom said it means Gift from God!" She said holding out her hand. Adam looked around and at the entrance and shook the girl's hand.

"Where is your mom, Jessica?"

"She's at the restroom. Do you want to say hello?" Adam raised himself quickly.

"Not right now. Perhaps some other time. It has been a pleasure Miss Jessica…"

"Goodbye Mr Adam." Jessica said to the sad man leaving the ward.

(Angels – Jessica Simpson) 64 741

Chapter Fifteen

They say, one percent inspiration, ninety-nine percent perspiration. I think it is the ninety-nine percent that comes before the floodgates of inspiration pour across the page, pen drying, quill scratching maniacally with not enough ink to satisfy the tidal wave of thoughts, expressions, and abstractions within us.

It appears to me that it is the creation of the seed which is the hardest of things. Once the seed is planted in whatever fertility we lay it in, watered and cared for, it grows and grows and flourishes and spreads out until there is no stopping the natural gush of its development. That seed could be a seed of creation, faith, hope, love, whatever you want it to be. Plant it, water it, protect it and watch it grow. Watch it flow like a fast-running stream gushing into a rapid flowing lake bounding over silt and rocks. Unhampered by obstacle. Unperturbed by geography. Watch it drop from high rocks and become the beautiful waterfall. The thick gathering foam below, swirling, before once again coursing forward. Let that seed grow into a beautiful tree, surrounded by other beautiful trees, until there is a thick, lush forest of imagination that dampens down any fire of destruction or devastation that dare come near. Creation, faith, hope and love flourishing like a thick green Amazon of the mind.

(Try Again – Aaliyah) 239 266

Nicholas and Jan settled at a large wooden table by the fire and began drinking at one of the only taverns that afforded such a service on a Sunday. As a result, the place was a local hub for sabbath insobriety. By the door, a religious man offered blessings and absolution to those that entered the premises, and his cup was always topped up with ale or wine depending on his preference.

"To your continued health my good friend!" Jan proclaimed as the two men clinked their drinking vessels together. "And to the sweet song of love and to the beautiful swans of its chorus…" Jan moved his hand in exaggerated animation around the room that was serving men and women alike. Nicholas laughed.

"Bravo." He said sinking large gulps of ale and scanning the room. Many were still dressed in their church attire and appeared less than concerned that it was the sabbath. Noisy men played cards and backgammon. Some were singing in a corner by the window and some of the women added their sweet chirruping to the deep tenor of the men. Jan looked over to where the men were singing: "Sea men, my friend…" He said gesturing to the group with his cup. "Paying homage to Nehallenia. … The sea dogs abound with salt in their bones. Sing to you fair lady, to carry us home."

"Pagans?" Jan raised his eyebrows and chuckled.

"Pagans, Christians… What is the difference, Nicholas? Men of faith. We all see God in our own ways…"

Nicholas took a gulp of his drink and looked away. "Ah, I see you don't agree, my friend!"

"There is only one Almighty in my opinion. The only one who offered up his only Son for our salvation." Jan downed his drink and leaned in closer to Nicholas.

"You see things… Too simply Nicholas. Too, how do you say? Black and white." Nicholas stared at Jan with eyes of ice blue, but the Dutchman was unmoved and continued: "There are two types of man. Men with faith, and men without faith. And how devoutly those second men cry!" Jan shook his head. "That is another subject altogether. To fight with another man over his own faith is to imagine the Gods are like humans with human intentions…"

Nicholas hailed an attendant to fill his cup and pointed to Jan's own empty cup. The woman poured and smiled at the men in their seriousness. Jan gestured to the woman with his head and patted Nicholas on the arm with a smile.

"Enough of this, Nicholas, today is for us, today we drink. Tomorrow God can have us." Nicholas nodded his head reluctantly and held up his cup to Jan who clinked it with his own.

(Lana Del Rey – Lust for Life) 178 411 177

The Man has been climbing for so long he has acclimatised to the altitude. Now he is lying in bed, next to his wife and he can't breathe. Something within him won't let go and he can't shake it. 'This is foolish, ridiculous, this is not right or real' every logical dissertation within him screams out. The essays of life laid out in clear black print on pristine pages of pure white flick through his brain in rapid succession. There is no precedence. No precedence! Later, on a deeper level, he argues for and against the actuality of there being no precedent, but for now, he turns over and closes his eyes and tries to sleep. Then turns again and turns again. The phrase runs through him like a cold wind and a warm Sun. A cool revitalizing sea wave lapping against him, within him, as he stands on a hot golden sand. He has sand in his eyelids and saltwater taste in his mouth that is stopping him from sleeping. He gets up. The feeling has him and he knows it won't abate until it is expressed. There will be no rainbow, no clear skies after the storm until he accepts, respects and expresses. He flicks open his laptop and writes for just a second before dropping the screen back down and heading back upstairs and drifting back to sleep. Before he does, he reasserts what his fingers had typed, just so every part of him is on the same page, and not some renegade part of him has taken over: "I Love You."

(Pink... The Color of Love - Yakuro) 2 321 090

Arabella and her friend Sara were walking past the tavern as the loud voices of the men reached the crescendo of their salty ballad.

"Let's go in!" Sara stopped and grasped the arm of her reluctant companion. "Come on! Come on!"

"For a short while, Sara, I'm serious." Arabella whined, dragging her feet behind her friend who was already through the entrance. After receiving their blessings, heads bowed, sign of the cross, they settled at a table by the serving area where a woman placed cups in front of them with a raise of the eyebrows.

"Ladies?"

"I'll have wine." Sarah chirruped. "Red." Arabella looked at her friend and back at the waitress who placed a hand on her waist.

"My Lady?" She mocked.

"I'll have wine too. White." Arabella returned assertively.

"Very good," and the waitress was off. A new song was starting in the corner as the waitress poured the drinks. Many of the throng that occupied the main area of the tavern began to join in and the waitress smiled as she also sang along cheerfully to herself. As she moved away, so did a group of men move into the corner to join the seafaring choir. Arabella watched as they moved away and a view of the fire appeared and a fair-haired man singing along, cup aloft, and a gentleman in black looking around unmoved but a little uncomfortable. He was not singing, because he was not Dutch. He was the stranger she had met earlier that day. She wanted to call out to him, but she remained silent, just watching him.

(If She Knew What She Wants – The Bangles) 5 877 645

It wasn't often that Nicholas felt out of place or in any state of vulnerability, but this was one of those occasions and he scanned the room uncomfortably. He had never seen such rowdiness and especially not in England on a Sunday afternoon. Jan was singing loud and in animated fashion and Nicholas watched as a group of men moved into the corner to sing with the protagonists of the Sunday merriment. Someone banged a table to his left and he watched as the men at the backgammon board shook their dice with purpose, blowing on their clasped hands, as if luck lay within their lungs. A man staggered through the centre of the tavern and fell keeping his cup aloft as a group at a table next to him laughed raucously and helped the man up who smiled appreciatively and sat at the table with them. Downing his drink and slamming it on the table in victorious fashion to rapturous applause from his new friends. Then he saw her. Across the room, opposite, looking at him then looking away quickly and talking to the dark-haired girl next to her. He kept his gaze on her and several moments later she returned it over the rim of her cup and their eyes locked. And space and time stood still, and the sound of the tavern dissipated - replaced by the rapid beating of his heart. He almost looked away because he felt his eyes dew up like they do in strong sunlight. Jan placed his drink on the table as the song was coming to a close and was about to engage with Nicholas until he saw his friend staring ahead in front of him and followed that stare to a fair-haired lady in a blue head scarf sipping from a cup at the table on the opposite side of the room. Jan nudged Nicholas roughly and brought him out of his trance and gestured his head in the direction of the lady. Nicholas looked away.

"Ah ha… Miss Pearls?" Nicholas took a large gulp of his drink.

"Miss Pearls." Jan looked over to where both girls were now looking over at them. Jan raised his cup: "Prost!" He shouted across the room.

(Ready or Not – The Fugees) 180 108 957

Chapter Sixteen

Have you ever seen someone cry like a baby behind their eyes? Like, all out bawling with a pain in the throat like turning balls of sand? No? Me neither, but it happens, because it happened to me, and I looked into the mirror to see if there was any outward show.

There wasn't. Just a lost, hopeless, look. I was at work and some hours later I walked out of work. I questioned my life, my purpose, my meaning, my idiotic thinking, and childish disillusions. Most of all I questioned the plan and that is something I should never do. Not because I am special or unique or of any particular favour of grace but because I made a conscious decision to trust in the process. To trust in a process that I have to sincerely believe is for the greater good and therefore my own minor role in it - my petty jealousies, my fragile pride – are of little significance to the mastery of the Universal show. I told myself to grow up and be a man; to own those feelings that we appear to have no control over and be a man about it. It is a moment, a dark moment in the eye of the storm. You and a mirror of your own feelings. Now you know they are there are you going to sit and pore over them in misery? Or are you going to step through the storm and try and perceive them in another way when the mind is clear again and the harsh conduit of insecurity is flushed out? The fact that the narrator is writing this would suggest the latter! Sometimes you just got to laugh with them. Sometimes you have to stop taking yourself so fucking seriously.

(Crying – Only Fools and Horses) 761 735

The Girl: "Why didn't I just tell him to Fuck Off in the beginning?"

The Man: "Why didn't she just tell me to Fuck Off in the beginning? Any normal person would have. She isn't just any normal, ordinary person though, is she…"

(Nothing Compares 2U – Sinead O'Connor) 284 753 313

In those first few weeks they called me, well some did, they called me Andy Dufresne. I didn't mind this appellation. Especially as he was the main character from my favourite film. And I got it. Quiet, aloof, perhaps a little cold with an untouchable aura. By the time I reached Healthcare I was more like the actual killer in the film. They say that for most new experiences the first few days are the hardest. Not with me here. In the first week I was moved to another Houseblock, another less permanent stage within the prison process. I actually didn't mind it here, the to-ing and fro-ing of different prisoners because of the relative shortness of their sentences, seemed to alleviate the consistent feeling of doom and gloom probably prevalent within the longer termers. Added to that I had the support of a friend from the outside who had recently been convicted for a one-year punch and had experience of the life and system, so he guided me through those early weeks until he was moved shortly before I was. I didn't have a job yet within the system and so I read, read as much as I could. I even intended to learn Latin but without adequate provisions yet built up and only a limited spend, despite my bank balance, I couldn't afford writing books and pens and all the other stuff required to seriously garner a learning skill. Eventually I was moved. My pad mate at the time cried. We had only known each other a week, but twenty-four hours seven days a week in the company of another person in that environment can seem a hell of a lot longer. So, I was moved to a 'better' block within the prison. It was so good at least two inmates said they thought I would 'string up' and these weren't even inmates that disliked me! If it was possible to snarl at people while holding your emotions in check, that is what I did.

"What do you mean?" I asked bemused.

"First timer, two and a half years..." They'd shake their head. "In here!" So, I ignored their ignorance of my character and carried on regardless. By the time I hit Healthcare I guess I had some understanding of what they meant.

(Marriage of Figaro – Shawshank Redemption) 1 881 977

Tobias had only seen his mother cry once before and that was following the death of his father. She wept for three days following the day on the hill where he watched the crazy cavalryman, the King, charge hopelessly across the field. On the fourth day a mysterious noble stranger, dressed in furs, with frills upon it of golden colour, visited their small home in the valley. Tobias was sent to his room as his mother prepared the man with provisions and they sat at their table, talking in hushed tones. Tobias crept out of his window and stroked the magnificent stallion belonging to the man tied up outside. He fed it the lush grass that grew in the valley and provided it with fresh water from the stream before climbing back into his room. He lay on his cot and tried to listen, nothing. So, he moved to a spot where he could see what was happening and determine what the stranger wanted with his mother. He watched as the man dropped a large bag onto the table in front of her, which she removed and placed in the larder. When she sat down, he leaned in close and as he reclined, he raised a finger at her, and he heard him say "Never!" The stranger raised himself and unclasped the sword belt from around his waist and placed it on the chair. His mother raised herself, hands together as if in prayer and bowed her head. The stranger placed a reassuring hand on her shoulder and was gone.

(Childhood's End – Marillion) 58 556

Adam pulled over his convertible beside the man carrying groceries along the sidewalk and pushed open the passenger door: "Get in Brian…"

Brian tossed his bag on the backseat and joined Adam in the car. "What is wrong with her?"

"If she doesn't get a donor soon, she is going to die! We have all took the tests, not one of us match. You are the only one in the family that we have not tried. It is not impossible to find a donor outside of the family, but the chances are slim…" Brian spent the rest of the journey explaining his granddaughter's condition to a sullen and solemn Adam. When they reached Brian's house

Adam turned to his brother who was gathering up his groceries from the backseat.

"I'll take the test. Tomorrow morning."

"Thank you." Brian turned to leave.

"One more thing, Brian." He turned to face his brother. "I want to meet her."

"Fine," Brian replied. "Tomorrow is her birthday, and we know you have already met her! She's an angel, isn't she?" Adam felt the tidal wave of emotion within him.

"Yes brother, she is!"

(Courage to Change – Color Music Choir) 692 023

Chapter Seventeen

There comes a point maybe in every man's life, maybe just some men's, maybe just mine, that you have to take the lid off the building. Scratch beneath the veneer and accept what is and has been without it needing to colour where you are going.

Obviously, a healthy respect of where you have come from, what you may or may not have done, what you said, what you didn't say, what you should have said are all part of the make-up that brings you to this moment in time. Sometimes that point may be a moment of crises, hopefully not, but wherever it brings you know that the next step doesn't have to be down the same sorry road. To walk that road takes courage and to change the road you have been and are walking takes courage still. Look up, look around and know that you are still present. Look up, look around and see the rain clouds disperse having watered the lush pastures that surround you. There, up ahead, is the rainbow! Follow it with Faith, Love and Hope in your heart. There is always the possibility that there will be Sunshine tomorrow.

(Colours of Love – Thomas Bergersen) 2 454

Jan nudged his new English friend: "Come, Nicholas, let us go and join the ladies!" Nicholas shook his head, but Jan had already picked up his cup and was heading over. Nicholas shook his head resignedly and followed Jan who was already introducing himself. "May we join you ladies? I'm Jan and this…" He said turning to Nicholas who joined him at his shoulder. "Is my learned friend from England, Nicholas." Arabella picked up her cup.

"We've already met." She said looking at Nicholas over the rim of her cup. Sara giggled and gestured to the unoccupied spaces opposite her and her friend.

"Merci." Jan said sitting opposite. "More drinks…" He said gesturing to the serving lady. "What are we drinking? Sara?" He peered into her cup. "Ah red wine, a religious girl." He said making the sign of the cross. "Bless you! And you Arabella?" She picked up her cup and showed it to Jan who was in full flow. "Ah, ah, white! Not so." Arabella placed her cup back on the table and without a flicker replied: "Anyone who knows the story of the crucifixion knows that Jesus bled both blood and water!" Jan sat back in his seat. "If red wine be the representation of blood, then could the white not be a representation of the unique and pure blood of Christ?"

With that Nicholas was in love and laughed loudly as he tapped Jan's foot with his stick. Jan laughed too.

"Bravo, young lady, bravo. I see why my friend is so captivated." Jan ordered the drinks with the serving lady who had just joined their table. Nicholas raised his cup and gestured it towards Arabella who returned the gesture with a smile.

(Red Red Wine – UB40) 162 352 741

Adam sat opposite the doctor in his office and waited, waited like a man waiting for his destiny to be revealed.

"I'm sorry Mr Cathcart," the doctor began. "You are not a match." Adam sat back in his chair and exhaled deeply.

"Okay, I see how this works!" Adam reached into the inside pocket of his jacket pocket and pulled out his cheque book and pushed it to the doctor opposite. "Put in a figure..." The doctor picked up the cheque book and angrily tossed it back over to Adam.

"With all due respect, Mr Cathcart, this is not one of your board rooms and I am not one of your employees that can be brow beaten into submission. You are NOT a match! Some things cannot be bought!" Adam sat forward in his chair and pushed the book back across. "Then find a fuckin' donor!" The doctor sighed.

"Look, I understand, I really do. I am a family man myself and would do anything for them any way that I could, and I realise that is what you are doing here Mr Cathcart."

Adam felt the imminence of a 'but' that would secure an anvil of defeat around his neck. He never lost at anything, but he knew he was about to. "Finding a donor is extremely rare and even then, there is no guarantee of success. Thank you for your time, Mr Cathcart, but this meeting is over. I wish you and your family well."

Adam lifted himself heavily from the chair and collected the three Disney character helium balloons he had brought for the niece he had yet to meet properly, their smiling happy faces a glowing contradiction to his feelings or the circumstance. He stopped at the door.

"This is not over. Not by a long way!"

(Purple, The Colour of Blood – Yakuro) 28 706

I don't even know whether that first week in healthcare was the worst, but I know it was bad. I think it got worse incrementally but when you've stood in one bad place it seems easier to deal with the next one. There were two cells on this particular block that were wide open to spectation and being a risk to one's own health I occupied one of them. An Officer sat outside watching you 24 hours a day. There was a brief reprieve – a small wall covered you for when you needed the toilet, but you were never really out of sight or earshot. Within a day or two I had smuggled cigarettes into the cell and when the craving killed me that is where I would smoke – blowing the exhalation into the basin. Every so often the Officer would shout: "Are you smoking?" "No, Boss!" Sometimes they said nothing. Life became sleep and sleep became life in those conditions. I would often sleep with my knees up while I was housed here, but of course that looked more suspicious than the simple fact that you just wanted to sleep unobserved so often you would hear the jangle of keys and the Officer peer over your bed to make sure you weren't up to no good. It was in this first week that I realised how deep a negative thought could take root in your brain and repeat, like the youngster that embarked on the nature adventure and came out with clothes covered in sticky weed. No matter how many you scraped off there were always some that remained. I tried to train my mind to steer clear, stray away, hold strong against travelling through the black abysses of the mind, the haunting caverns of the brain, but the more I resisted, the more it pulled me in. I lay there one night and felt like my arms and legs were being pulled as if they were on pieces of string and as I felt and attempted to analyse this strange bodily phenomenon I could hear whispering voices, nothing coherent, external not internal, whispering voices that may or may not have been there. I remember it reminded me of the Cruciatus spell demonstrated by Mad Eye Moody in one of the Harry Potter films. My tortured body being manipulated by the cruel intentioned wand of another, a machine that could achieve such a task, locked up and kept out of sight in one of the rooms in healthcare. At that time, I had a face and name for the perpetrator, it was another prisoner on the block I had left. It was of course an impossibility. A screeching chasm between fantasy and reason. By the time I left, shipped out of healthcare, the perpetrators, the apparitions of my torture, had evolved to a level beyond any reasonable proportion.

(Adagio for Strings/Secret – Tiesto) 13 283 635

Adam moved slowly through the hospital, balloons in hand, hoping today would be a celebration. A chance for him to really do something for someone else. He entered the ward and when he reached the door to her room he stopped and composed himself. His many years in business and in constant face to face contact with associates and clients that required his confidence, his reliability, had taught him the art, had made him a master of facial subterfuge. So, he painted upon his face a smile of radiance, the smile of a man, a great uncle, that had come to visit his niece on her birthday. He knocked on the glass and quickly entered with false gusto. His brother was sat by the window, Amy occupied a seat by the bed where Jessica sat cross-legged amid pictures strewn upon it.

"Happy Birthday Young Lady!" He announced holding aloft the large balloons in his possession, large smile upon his face. Jessica leapt off the bed, close to tears and into the arms of her mother, who stroked back her hair and was soothing her daughter: "It's okay, baby, it's okay." Adam's face flushed white, drained of all colour.

"I'm so sorry… I'll…" The girl looked at him, then turned it and buried it into the breast of her mother.

"It's not you Adam…" Amy said. "It's the balloons. She has a fear. Will you take them out please?"

"Good God, of course! I'm so sorry!" Adam quickly exited the room and stood uselessly in the middle of the ward holding the balloons. Brian followed and put a hand on his brother's shoulder.

"It's okay brother you weren't to know." Adam sat heavily and sighed.

"I'm not a match Brian. I'm so sorry, I'm not a match." Brian sat next to Adam who had stooped in his chair and patted his back.

"It's okay, Adam, we knew it was a long shot, but we had to try. You did what needed to be done brother. That is all any of us can do." Adam looked across to his brother, eyes watering up.

"How do you? How…" Brian smiled patiently and made a gesture with his eyes that suggested incredulity.

"What else are we to do?" He stood up. "We love her with everything in our heart. That is what we do. Give the balloons to the nurse, she will soon find a home for them, then come and meet her."

When Adam left an hour later there were children running around the ward laughing joyfully. A mermaid and a blonde girl dressed in blue who was apparently called Elsa were being chased by a young, kind, and re-gal looking Lion. When he caught them, he turned and was chased by them. Adam smiled as he left the ward.

(The Circle of Life – The Lion King 2019) 1 150 602

Chapter Eighteen

In the end it comes down to a choice. Get busy living and die trying.

Healthcare was my war. The space between my ears the muddy, hopeless, tracts of wet thick wasteland between the trenches of the Somme, of Verdun. The deep, open space of my heart was the Blitz and the Battle of Britain. Running for cover until there was no more cover. My soul was fought on the hills and the meadows, amidst the trees and the farmhouses of Waterloo. The real problem with war is that even when there is a victor, only history will tell if it is a real victory. One thing is sure. All wars leave scars.

(Feel – Mahmut Orhan) 33 231 367

The Man is sat on a chair in his observation cell. They can't see what he is doing, just that he is doing something. They probably don't really care; the people down here are a little crazy anyway. He has packs of sugar, whitener and other objects of little real consequence on their own. It is only when you apply your own metaphor to them that they become significant. He is shuffling them about with purpose but without any real purpose because the act itself has no purpose. He is searching his memory, tracing every footstep of his time in this place, and he is making a plan of the prison with his little bag of supplies. They can't see because he is doing it on a shelf on the cupboard provided and then he gets the feeling, the feeling he once experienced when under the influence of LSD and he was playing Monopoly, but this time he doesn't lose consciousness. This feeling would visit him again some weeks later, still in healthcare, when he was playing chess with a friend during recreation time. Like a wave, a surge, rising through him and feeling like he was observing himself or some world from his Crown Chakra. Some years later, whilst at work, he hasn't been taking his pills, he looks out onto the factory floor before him, through his window and sees the Universe in all its glory. He doesn't remember losing consciousness, more an absent-mindedness and he has lost four minutes and he is loading his table from the opposite end.

(Sail Away [Ploxy Remix] – Enya) 1 902 026

Adam lay in his bed awake. He hadn't bothered to roll down the shutters to his windows, maybe wouldn't again, and the summer moon poured a sliver of silver light across his bed. He was remembering the afternoon, with his estranged family and the girl within it that had lit his heart.

When he re-entered the room on the ward Jessica was back on her bed. "I'm so sorry, Young Lady, I hope I haven't ruined your day!?" Jessica dropped off the bed and walked up to Adam with her hand outstretched to him, which took him a little by surprise, but he took it anyway.

"Hello, my name is Jessica... It is a pleasure to meet you." She looked at her mother. "Great..." Amy nodded. "Great Uncle Adam." His heart was melting like a smiling snowman in a hot noon sun.

"The pleasure is all mine, Jessica. Did you get lots of nice things for your birthday?" She ran around to her bedside cabinet and called out excitedly: "Would you like to see!?"

"Sure."

She opened up the cabinet and pulled out paints and felt pens and colouring books and a blank sketchbook and placed them on the bed.

"These are off grandad and so are these," she said, picking up a packet of crayons that lay on the bed. "And these wax ones!" She pointed to the wax crayons dotted about on the bed, the obvious choice of her latest project.

"Ah, so you are a budding Van Gogh then?" Jessica looked at her grandad who was looking out of the window.

"Picasso!" He said, without looking around. Jessica chuckled.

"Grandad says my faces are like Picasso." Adam moved over to where her art was littered all over the bed.

"Oh yes, I see… That one there must be your mother, is it?" He said looking towards Amy who raised her eyebrows and smiled.

"Mommy says that one is interesting. Is interesting good, Uncle Adam?"

"Interesting is very good, Jessica, very good indeed." He laughed and sat on the bed. "Without interest there is no interest!" Jessica pulled a face of perplexity and went back into the cabinet.

"Do you want to see what I got off Mommy and Daddy?"

"Absolutely!"

She pulled out an oblong velvet box and opened it up and passed it to Adam. It was a silver heart shaped pendant with Jessica written on the front. He turned it around and in quotation marks was written: "Gift from God." He felt his throat constrict and the water of his well filling up.

"That's beautiful," he said, fingers shaking as he turned the pendant back around. "Be sure to look after something as precious as that..." He handed the box back to her and her eyes became serious.

"That's why it's still in the box uncle Adam!" He laughed.

"Apart from the wonderful presents you already have... What else would you like? If you could have anything?" Amy leaned forward in her chair about to speak and looked at her father who shook his head almost imperceptibly to his daughter who sat back and shot Brian 'we'll talk later' eyes.

"Duh, a penguin!" Jessica fired straight at the man who erupted in laughter along with Brian and Amy.

"A real one?" He asked incredulously.

"Yeah," she said, jumping back on the bed. "I'm drawing one... Look!" He spent an hour in the company of his remarkable great niece and now he lay thinking, thinking, plotting.

(Winter in July – Sarah Brightman) 39 672

I think I can bookmark my time in healthcare as the time the signs first gained a momentum of proportions beyond my control. As a result, self-sabotage, and a ruthless assassination of one's own character, became a daily occurrence behind the dim lamps of my eyes. Sometimes in the company of others, sometimes not. The signs had only just begun when I first met the doctor. I can't remember whether it was within the first week or not, but I had already begun to scan a room for them. Pictures, writings, anything that could provide a metaphor. The doctor sat opposite me, across the large table, in the room the patients would consult about the current state of things within the environment and within themselves to a finger or two of nurses or other experts such as psychologists. Behind me was a large glass window, behind which, was the nurses station. Today there were officers and nurses in the room itself. Not necessarily watching me, but there, nevertheless. I was talking to the doctor, explaining about the symptoms of my condition, the signposts of my anxiety, when he began scratching his eyebrow with just his middle finger, just like we all used to do at school. I actually stopped talking, I think I may have even cocked my head, open-mouthed; may even have shrugged my fucking shoulders. I must have been talking about the signs because I remember saying: "You're doing it now!" (What I didn't say was: and not with any subtlety you dumb fuck!) I felt as if behind me they were laughing, were they laughing? They may have been laughing, but not at you! He of course acted with surprise and assured me he had not the slightest realisation of what he had been doing, merely that he had an itch. On another occasion, I think my breakdown had reached a severity that demanded the attention of one of the prison Warders and half a dozen other officials I had never seen or see again. This time we were sat in the rec room at a long table with myself at one end scrutinised by these people. I don't remember, I can't give an accurate account of the actual interview, (interrogation?) that took place. What I do remember is that at its conclusion the Warder said brusquely: "Do we have anything here?"

What did that even mean? All eyes turned to him as if I didn't exist like some hunched husk on a chair before them. 'Yes, you have something here Warder! You have a man in pieces held together only by the glue of those memories of those that loved him, that love him still!' Those were the interactions within this environment that I can account for with any real fact. The rest was just conjecture.

(What's Going On – 4 Non Blondes) 1 193 643 687

Laying on bed, torch lit, walking the dark chasms of the mind. Every rock in the deep cavern had a signpost attached: 'Lift Me!' Like a dutiful lower vibrational self, I obeyed, and such are the morbid dark delights of a brain bent on the purification of its own memory. That is of course sarcasm. This is of course no self-help course with pretty words and pretty metaphors except when you eventually realise something about yourself that only such a course can enlighten. Sometimes our willingness to hurt ourselves can be strong but our cast iron will to survive is so much stronger. In that cell, call it what you will, light and dark, God and the Devil, the polarities of every part of me clashed in a duel of epic proportions. Paranoia of continual observation was a hysteria that held sway throughout my stay here and the light and dark became the original earpieces to my confessions. With nothing but my own memories for company, that is where I holed up. The outside world in this place, a projection, as if I was observing it through my eyes as windows on a world I had no intention of participating in. If I was dying before I came in here, I was now laying in death's coffin feeling as if I was being judged by forces far stronger than Man's mediocre and parochial opinions and judgements.

A guy on the ward looked at me once and said: "Think positive!"

I tiredly smiled back at him and said: "I'm trying…"

But it was impossible here. Sometimes I would go through the cavern and see fingers of light, I was winning, laying there, prostrate, but manoeuvring through my mind with purpose. Sometimes I would hear the Officers bang loudly in the nurses' station as an affirmation to the success of my current journey and then one thought would roadblock the journey and I heard the groans as loudly as if they were stood around my bed observing me. On more than one occasion in the rec room, deeply entrenched in my own mind, perhaps going well, flying, and then a voice would come in and shot a nuke in there. I would watch as the Officers coming in and out of the recreation room would sigh loudly and drop their heads. That, I believe, is where the idea that I was attached to a mind-reading machine was born.

(It's You, Not Me (Sabotage) – Bebe Rexha) 320 005

Laying in that bed, day and night, with only my own tiring thoughts for company, it wasn't long before Judas arrived. The pretext was simple: I betrayed a friend and with the mania rampant I couldn't just see it at the face value of what it was. It had to be epic. Betrayal of a friend at the highest echelon. The truth was, verbally, I never betrayed anyone to anyone. In this place, you learned that code of honour very early on. Snitches get stitches was not just some frivolous phrase here. People actually moved to the worst place one could be in this the darkest of places just to escape the consequence of their own mouths. You had a problem you had to deal with it yourself. The problem I had was the deep-seated feeling that I was being observed, either by a higher or lower vibrational power and if they had access to my mind, then I had betrayed. Judas occupied at my lowest moments, the moments of my weakest and most vulnerable. I don't remember the exact question I asked the ether when the kettle turned itself on, but I suspect it was something Judas related. When I repeated the question again and the kettle once again boiled, I took hold of the kettle placed my left hand, pinned it with my will to the bottom of the sink, and poured the full contents of the boiled kettle upon it. It was over a day before anyone realised what I had done. It wasn't their fault - I kept it well hidden from them - despite the yellow ballooning of the skin on my hand. I remember the chief nurse dressing the messed wound of my left claw when they finally discovered the severity of it, I had been popping the pus-filled wounds of the ballooning with a pen, and she said, there were tears welled-up in her eyes: "You don't have to do this you know..." By then my mind had betrayed many, a lot of the time with invented truths. When the officers took me to the hospital for a second time to have the wound dealt with, I sincerely believed I was going to be executed in the back of the transport en route. When I had survived that journey, I believed I was going to be executed in a public square behind the hospital. A phone call came to the reception, a reprieve, I was granted a mercy. With hindsight and logic what I have come to realise is that it took several seconds for the kettle to boil, meaning it was already in the process before the pertinent question was asked! What I originally thought of as a supernatural event may of course have not been that at all.

(The Boxer – Simon and Garfunkel) 23 560 109

Epsilon and his family moved away from the water point and into the jungle to shelter from the incoming rain. His new-born daughter clung to her mother and his son walked by his side. A storm that had passed through over the last couple of days hampered their usual access into the canopy of the jungle and so they had to use another route. A route, as yet unexplored. Their destination was of course the shelter of the large forest tree Epsilon first felt the real warm embrace of the Sun. They were not too far into the foliage when Epsilon noticed the monkey that made its way at speed towards them. Epsilon stopped and ushered his family behind him and into the protective shelter of the jungle canopy. He backed up against the trunk of a tree as the screeching of the monkey tearing towards him began, but he held steadfast, maintaining his position against the tree. His son moved beside but he pushed him back as the ape appeared before him hollering and snarling, baring dangerous and purposeful teeth. The whole area teemed with the noise of Alpha and his horde as the main ape moved before Epsilon from left to right never taking his eye off the monkey that had wandered accidentally into his area. Epsilon remained on hands as the Alpha continued his display of aggression in front of him, never breaking eye contact. When Alpha raised himself off hands and stood over Epsilon, he countered by doing the same and with the two rocks in hand, which he now always carried with him, he slammed together his hands. An errant orange light drifted through the air to a shocked looking Alpha as the light buried itself into his fur and set up the hair around his chest like a wildfire. The panic-stricken cries of the aggressor seemed to silence the hollering of the other monkeys that were around and stayed and watched as he frantically beat out the affliction imposed upon his chest. Epsilon watched as the aggression drained from Alpha's eyes and he dropped himself back onto his hands. With the flame out Alpha continued to holler at the intruder but with a passion extinguished like the flame that had risen around his chest. He moved backwards and forwards in front of Epsilon, the eye contact remaining, but the noise in his lungs becoming duller and duller until it was almost mute. Alpha moved slowly back to his place under his tree, turning once to see Epsilon turn and usher his family onward into the thick canopy of the jungle.

(Adiemus – Lord of the Rings) 37 120 757

It wasn't all doom and gloom and the sorry dark vision of conceivably history's biggest betrayer. There were personages I imagined being within these walls that were entertaining and situations likewise. One day a small army of crows had gathered outside of my window. At the time, I didn't have any idea of the symbolic and spiritual duality portrayed by the crow and its family of black birds. At this time in space, in this place, they were not the best of omens, and I willed them away. Away from my window, away from me. All of a sudden, a squadron of seagulls swooped and moved the crows off and chased them in a battle of Britainesque display of aerial combat. At that time there were a number of reports of seagull's venturing further into human territory, stealing from shops, daring raids on food in the hands of their food chain superiors. In my head it was a growing consciousness, an evolution, a brazen fearlessness. I watched for several minutes as the seagulls and crows swirled and glided in their natural glory of flight and celebrated the victory of the seagull over its winged counterpart.

(I'll Fly with You – Gigi D'Agostino) 18 818 032

In my time here I had taken on the identities, unwillingly of course, of the dark figures of Ghost Rider,

Batman; the heroic personality of Neo, even Morpheus; and the evolutionary form of super ape, Caesar. By then I believed the observers were from the far reaches of space who had come to realise my ability to communicate, if only with myself, on some completely different level. One night in a trance of euphoria of indecipherable description I made peace with the whole world, even the victims of my crime, and made a speech in my head of such glorious clarity and appeasement that when I came out of the trance, I expected my prison door to be unlocked. I even checked. Of course, it wasn't! Sometimes in the ether of my imagination I could hear my mother and auntie talking to me. Always quite good at the unravelling of anagrams, that were constant within the confines of my mind, I don't remember if it was sometime after or during my time here, I unravelled one that must have sent a shiver or gave some semblance of comfort to the broken. My Mother's maiden name when rearranged spelt: 'God ran jail.' Always a keen scholar of the Mythological, it wasn't long after the Greeks arrived that I was shipped out of Fantasy Island.

(The Boxer – Alison Krauss & Shawn Colvin) 2 948 972

It appears blasphemy and hubristic behaviour are more likely to get you shipped out of prison and into the loony bin quicker than any action of self-harm, even if that action is pouring a full kettle of boiling water on your hand. I didn't know whether I was God, one of the Gods, or a combination, but just that the mention of 'God Complex' had a representative of Roseberry Park interviewing me. It wasn't at any great length but what I had said had had me recommended for the move. Perhaps it wasn't what I had said but the way in which I had said it or acted, as if I truly and entirely believed it. It wasn't an act. I did, and the idea of it distressed me no end. How could someone so flawed be a God? I wasn't brought up on any religion of any kind, it didn't live and breathe within the four walls of my home growing up but sometimes when the man, laying in his bed thought like this, he half expected a forearm to come up through the bed, lay across his stomach, and pull him through the bed to some unknown realm. The forearm never came and a week or two later, despite the stigma associated with the place, he had more freedom than he could ever have conceived within the terms of a prison sentence.

(One of Us – Joan Osborne) 9 557 540

Chapter Nineteen

Peace. What is it to have peace? And what is peace anyway? Is it the harmony that is felt within the carrier that seems to indicate that everything is okay, more than okay, but good? Okay within themselves, within the parameters of their control?

It is perhaps an acceptance that the peace of mind I myself sought to achieve at the beginning of the year has everything to do with everything that lies within me and not in anyone else. Their whims, their passions, their feelings or lack of are nothing to do with sustaining a personal peace of mind, but merely an external factor we imagine will balance the chemical set of our brains; still or even stir the waters of our emotions. Peace of mind may merely be the realisation that we are the captain and crew of our own ship on the wide vast Ocean of our own existence. Whether we bring anyone on board secondary to the true meaning of an inner peace that many of us seek, that the ebbs and flows of the waters we sail on are all down to ourselves! It would be a lie, personally, to suggest that external factors do not play any role, particularly in the harmony of one's peace. But it is also a lie to suggest that sometimes the disharmony and discord we think, and feel is impossible to fix without the aid of external factors. When we look at the Earth in simplistic terms we are provided, as a human species, everything that is required for our bodies to survive, to live comfortably even, to thrive. Is it impossible to conceive that as children of the Earth we are not granted the same resources within the confines of our own walking, talking planet to survive, live in comfort and thrive on a mental, emotional and spiritual level?

(Alright – Supergrass) 13 989 030

The landlord was in the hallway of Irene Cathcart's house gesticulating and pleading desperately as she stood blowing smoke in his direction.

"Please, Irene, please call your son. This is getting out of hand!" He gestured to a letter he held in his left hand. "He is a rich man, Irene, a rich man!" Irene Cathcart looked nonchalantly at the frantic little man who put the letter on a table.

"Get out of my house." She asserted. "And close the door on your way out!" The man shook his head walking backwards towards the door and put his hands together as if in prayer: "Please, make the call. Make the call Irene." Despite every indication to the man that she wouldn't she did make the call anyway and Adam was round within the hour. They were sat at the kitchen table across from each other.

"Will you loan me the money?" She said, not looking at Adam, until she had lit her cigarette. "Yes. It's not a loan. Can we talk about Dad?" She looked away and blew out a long channel of cigarette smoke.

"Have you got the money with you?"

"Yes. Ma?"

"All of it?" Adam sighed and took out an envelope which contained the rent money she owed and placed it on the plastic tablecloth. He shrugged his shoulders and pointed his palms towards her: "Mother!?"

"I take it I don't have to count it…" He raised himself up from the table and looked into her eyes.

"Two thousand three hundred dollars!" He turned and made his way towards the kitchen door and had his hand on the handle.

"Adam?" She called out weakly. He turned. "Your father was always devoted to you boys. He always loved you. That never stopped." His eyes weakened. She pulled out another cigarette and lit it. She kept her eyes on the cigarette, rolling it in her fingers as she continued: "I stopped him from seeing you." She took a long drag and blew out the cigarette smoke as she looked straight at her son. "I knew that was the only thing I could do to hurt him. I knew that would destroy him." Adam Cathcart shook his head. "When he left me for her, he took my heart with him." She placed the cigarette in the ashtray and watched the swirling blue smoke. "When your father died. My heart died with him too!" A tear dropped onto the plastic cloth with a loud splatter as her son felt a rage grow in his body from his feet to his mouth and off his tongue.

"I hope God can forgive you Reenee. I hope he is merciful and full of fuckin forgiveness. Because I can't forgive you!"

"I know, son, I know." The little woman said looking at the angry man before her.

"I've led a life free of relationship because I feared they would be just like you!" The tears began to free fall onto the tablecloth.

"I know that too, Adam, I know that too and I'm sorry."

"You get short again call me..." He left the rest unsaid, then pulled open the kitchen door and slammed it behind him. As he reached the hallway Brian was entering the front door and the brothers eyed each other like grudge match heavyweights.

"What are you doing here?" Brian demanded as they passed.

"None of your fuckin business!" Adam replied as he stormed from the house.

Gazing at the screen of his computer Adam was thinking of this moment, about his father and his mother, and the tears they fell for them, but mostly they fell for the little girl his body couldn't save.

(Bohemian Rhapsody – Queen) 1 428 922 465

The Man and his sister were sat around her large front room table, both leathered from the night's drinking. It was either the night of her funeral or the night we knew she wasn't leaving the hospital. There had been tears and there had been honesty; not least the worries that had plagued his mind over the past few months. He knew his sister was the only person that would listen that wouldn't laugh or mock him or want to have him committed. They were on the gin by this time, and he was relaying a story about how sat in his cell in healthcare one dark night a journey had begun which resulted in him sat watching the cell door and waiting for it to open to reveal the one person in the world he would like to punch. It took a while, perhaps all night, to arrive at his conclusion. At the time he figured all the inmates on the block were going through the same thing, like running some kind of emotional or spiritual gauntlet. There has to be someone that you would a voice in his head said and so he sat waiting for his father. His sister cried. She cried hard. He put out his hand on her arm and remonstrated, trying to alleviate the feelings of love and loyalty that must have clashed within her.

"You are getting me wrong." He continued. "It isn't because I hate dad, I love my dad, I felt I had to choose, like I had no choice." He took a large gulp of gin. "And I know dad would take it off me. Dad would take it away from me if he could. That is why. That is the only reason why!" Her tears subsided and she said something that surprised him.

"Do you know what he said to me? Last time, last time I went to see him?" The Man listened. "He said, of all of his children, you are the one he worries about the most because you are so clever!" The Man shook his head and protested as he remembered his junior school years and always being behind on his work programme or kept back after school because he couldn't solve a simple arithmetic problem.

"I was never that clever. I just tried. Sometimes, I would just want to try." Then she told me about a dream she had had. The horror of it and how she had dealt with it and: "At the end there was you being dragged across a beach. You weren't struggling."

"Did I protest?"

"No, far from it, you were smiling!"

"Then don't worry about it then, Sis. It is just love. I am just being dragged away by love…"

(November – Max Richter) 15 834 777

Many things changed for Tobias after the visiting stranger. His mother stocked up the larder with fresh meat and fish and vegetables in a fashion he had never experienced before. She stopped him from going to school, an event which perplexed him, especially given his mother's views on the importance of a good education, but not something he complained about. He knew that something was going on, something that could heed his whole world crashing down, but she remained silent about it for the time being. Despite the stock of food already acquired by his mother he spent his days fishing by the stream, enjoying the hiatus and would bring the big fish he caught back home. A week after the stranger had come by his mother announced over supper that they were to move away. Far away from here. The silence was finally broken and felt like an errant crashing wave. Tobias protested, but to no avail. His mother had been quite adamant that no amount of persuasion, protestation or manipulation would make her change her mind. "Where? Where are we going?" He had shouted as he made his way to his room and laid sulking on his bed. His mother followed and ushered for him to follow her. She pulled out a stool to the table and beckoned for him to sit down while she busied herself in the larder. He sat, head in his hands and elbows on the table when his mother returned and he heard the clank of metal being dropped, carefully, onto the tabletop. He turned his head to see a sword, sheathed in leather upon a leather belt, placed on the table in front of him. He looked at his mother and she nodded with assent as he gripped the handle tightly and slowly pulled the weapon from the sheath. He pulled it only a little way out, his eyes wide with amazement. He looked at his mother questioningly and she nodded again: "Yes, Tobias, it is yours!" Tobias beamed with excitement, his eyes full of joy and his mouth full of questions.

"From the man? The man with the horse?" His mother frowned and put her hand down on the table firmly as she fixed her son with a stern gaze.

"Tobias, you must never mention that man again. Do you hear me?"

"But…"

"Tobias!" She reasserted. "Do. You. Hear. Me!?"

"Yes Mother." He said, disgruntled, before continuing to inspect the splendid weapon in front of him. Just below the handle was an engraving of a leafed stalk with three flowers drooping from it. He ran his fingers over the engraving.

"Ask me, then never mention it to anyone else again?" His mother said, watching her fascinated son.

"What is it? And what does it mean?"

"It is a sprig of broom. It symbolises good luck and the warding off of evil. It also symbolises courage and resourcefulness, qualities you will need." Tobias looked at his mother. "In a few days we are moving far from here. North. To a place called York. You, Tobias, my son, are going to be a great soldier!"

(Secrets - Tiesto feat Vassy) 250 292 068

Over the past few years Robert's mood swings had calmed to the point where his father felt it apt that he should tutor him himself in the intricate study, repair, maintenance, and construction of timepieces. It appeared he was a natural with a passion for the trade that matched his fathers. It even opened up further doors of education that once would have seemed alien to the boy of a few years previous. He read voraciously, everything to do with mathematics. His artistic drawings of the various mechanics of the clock and watch were exquisitely executed on any bits of paper he could get his hands on. There were even little drawings of his own design with numbers and arrows in relation to the main body of the mechanics. They baffled his father, but they kept him stable and kept him grounded so his father never voiced his perplexity. This morning he was up before the Sun, his father and the cock crow. Candle lit he was looking through a magnifying glass at the latest repair that had come into the shop, sketching and numbering on a piece of scrap paper, the minute devices of the watch as they pulsed and turned. When he was finished, distracted, ordering the new drawings into his head, he blew out the candle and was about to take a step towards his room when he felt the sharp jar of one of his father's small tables hit him in the thigh. He felt the gravity of the table shift away and heard the pin drops of tiny devices hit the stone floor before the heavy thud of wood hitting floor.

"No!" He whispered silently. Then he burst. "NOOOOOOOOO! FATHER! NOOOOOOOOO! JACQUES! JACQUES!"

The flickering orange of a frantic candle entered the room.

"Robert! Robert! What is it my boy?" The young man fell to the floor with his hands over both ears looking at the damage he had caused. The innards of several watches scattered across the floor in front of him.

"LOOK!" He cried. "LOOK what I have done!" His father scampered over to his desolate son and kneeled by his side and took hold of his head in his hands.

"Robert? Robert! Look at me! It's okay my boy…" He lit the other candle. "Take this Robert. Take it." His father picked up the table and started assembling the pieces of the timepieces back onto his table. "Come on. Help me." His son obeyed but his face was ashen white.

He picked up the pieces silently, like the whole of his spirit had diminished into a tiny box within himself. "I think we got them all. No panic my son, no panic." He put his hand on the side of Robert's sullen face. "It's okay, Robert, it's okay!" His son removed his father's hand. Picked up the piece of paper he had been drawing on and headed heavily towards his room. "You don't understand," he said. "Nobody understands."

(Disorder – Joy Division) 19 953 195

Moving from the Big House, as my auntie referred to it, into the loony bin, as we all as kids used to call this place, I now found myself in was like dropping from a huge height into a massive pile of marshmallows. Liberalism and the bleeding, beating heart view that people should be repaired, not dungeoned at its best. This foray back into a world of humanity undoubtedly settled within me the strength to see out the remainder of the sentence. The ward held six of us and two of them I already knew from healthcare. One of those, was my best friend as far as it could be called that in such an environment, from healthcare. He did used to say to me often, in the small yard of healthcare, that this destination was his plan. They give you money, as many visits as you like (and they can bring stuff in for you!), takeaways a few days a week he used to say to me, and I would look at him like he was in a fantasy world. He'd wink at me and say: "I'm two steps ahead of them! I'm an Illuminati foot soldier…" He'd confide and then showed me a big tattoo on his calf of the triangle with the eye and he'd wink again. They think I'm crazy, he'd laugh. I'd laugh, thinking he was crazy. So now we were re-united in this place. And guess what? What he had said about this place… He was right, every word.

(Play The Game – One Flew Over the Cuckoo's Nest)
71 937

As the latest song came to a close, Jan slapped Nicholas on the back, possibly a little more aggressively than was courteous. The ale was clearly taking effect: "My friend, let us swap places. I don't think your Miss Arabella likes me too much!" Nicholas raised himself and walked around to the right of Jan who slid across onto the seat that had become occupied, taking hold of it and moving it around to the end of the table and closer to Sara. "Besides I would like to know more about this divine creature!" He said, looking at Sara who giggled girlishly. Nicholas sat and faced Arabella.

"Hello again."

"Hello."

"I expected to run into you again but not so soon." Nicholas laid his cane across the table. "Providence perhaps," Arabella said sipping her drink. Nicholas put his hands together in exaggerated prayer and looked up to the heavens before back at Arabella who chuckled. She put down her drink and her elbow on the table to lean in closer to the English man. "You are a man of God Nicholas," she began. "What are you doing in a place like this?" She was looking around at the sights around her and Nicholas turned to take in the scene

himself. "Probably the same reason you are Arabella."
She thought for a second.

"Curiosity?"

"Perhaps."

"Because your friend dragged you in here?" Nicholas
laughed and looked at Jan who was intimately whispering into the ear of Arabella's friend.

"I'm impressed Miss Arabella. You read minds?"
She shook her head and nodded in the direction of Sara.
Nicholas picked up his cup and drank. "And maybe a
little pleasure." Arabella picked up her own cup and offered it towards Nicholas who clinked it. "I don't believe it is the nature of God to deprive man of pleasure,
basic or otherwise. It is a man's purpose to find God in
his own way!"

"And a woman's?" Arabella said a little testily.

"Ah, the swans."

"Excuse me…"

"Nothing, my dear, just something Jan said earlier
about the women of your blessed nation." Arabella
looked across at Jan who now had his hand on top of her
friend's hand.

"He said women were swans?" She looked at Nicholas.

"Dutch women… He was quite specific."

"Swans traditionally have one partner for life do they not?" Nicholas thought for a second then leaned in.

"Yes, Arabella, I believe they do!"

(Entrance of Swans – Swan Lake) 2 468 585

Chapter Twenty

Several years ago, my mind broke and every day from that moment to this has been spent attempting to put the fragmented pieces back together.

Not only that. I hold the fragmented pieces in my hand and view them and scrutinize them with a keen and astute eye, before fixing them together like an avid jigsaw puzzler. Some of the pieces don't even appear to belong to the puzzle I am reconstructing. I noticed that some years ago not long after the fragmentation. Little narratives and stories of memories that never happened and don't belong. Preternatural images that had no place, except that in the dark spaces that surrounded like a fog, locked in the cold hard walls of the place, even the surreal had its place as if the non-acceptance of both the beauty and the horror would take your head spinning. Feeling like the head would start a tic at a thousand miles an hour and the only relief from the madness of it was to take yourself out of the walls of your headspace. Now the pieces lay, observable and reconstructable, with the pieces that don't belong there disintegrating in the hands like calcified horse shit.

(Never Give Up – Sia) 120 868 559

Robert found his father, Jacques, dead three days after the incident in his workshop, exactly seventy-two hours later. He knew it was to the hour because he noted the time on a clock in the workshop when his father entered that night with a candle. Now the candle in his father's room flickered bright orange and almost life-like in the dark and silence of the room. He bent over the bed and almost fell backwards in fright at the shadow that loomed over his eternally sleeping father, until he realised that the shadow was his own, with thin elongated fingers accentuated on the whitewash walls. "Father! Father! FATHER!" He bent in but heard no breathing. He shook the man, but he remained asleep. He touched his skin, and it was as cold as winter gutter water. Now he sat and took his father's skilful hands in his own and rocked back and forth wondering what to do next. Three days after his father's death, while he was padding about barefoot in the workshop, not knowing exactly what it was he was doing there, he felt a sharp stabbing in the sole of his foot and lifted it to reveal a sharp but minute mechanism that had been the only piece they could not find from the incident six days before. Robert had spent the following few days looking for the piece without success. Now it sat lodged in his foot and then in the pinch of his fingers. He viewed it with nonchalant fascination before putting it in the pocket of his nightdress. Three days after that his father was buried in a small but nearby Catholic church. Nine days from the incident to the expiration, two hundred and sixteen hours, in the year of our Lord one-six-six-six. A small gathering of his father's friends stood around the open mouth of the grave when the young man shouted stop and pulled open the lid to Jacque's final resting place. "Robert! What are you doing!" The men cried to the young man who bent down and whispered into his dead father's ear before placing the missing mechanism in his hands and prising closed the stiff fingers of the departing corpse.

(Prelude No 4 – Chopin, Khatia Buniatishvili) 1 394 499

The Man is wrapped within his quilt like the sausage in a sausage roll – but his mind is in the thorn bushes of his thoughts. It is January and he has just found out, maybe hours, maybe days before, that the mother of his eldest daughter is not going to leave her hospital bed. He doesn't know how he got here, but he is here anyway, he is the Polar Ice Caps. He didn't ask for this and this is the last thing he wants to be at this moment in time because he wants to break, he wants to melt, he wants to surrender and let the whole of him flood out. But he doesn't, he can't, what sure catastrophe would there be should he melt? So, he lies there, fighting the thoughts that have put him here and not a single teardrop falls, not one layer of his heart melts. He is a rock.

By February, she has died, and the sometimes-volatile relationship between the Man and his daughter has reached a point where they are barely speaking. She is wilful and he is proud, a combination that leaves little room for compromise and without the loving common sense of the common denominator between them, except of course genetics, the idea of a reconciliation looks tenuous. He has shed tears now, big bell-bottomed tears that fell rapidly like a waterfall onto his keyboard, when he made a video, a tribute, dedicated to her on the night of the day of her death. Now he is standing outside the funeral parlour, shaking hands with three of the four men, other than himself, that she ever loved all waiting to pay their last respects. Her family have gone in already and so too has his daughter, so there is no chance to give her any warm words or strong words of encouragement. He leads the rest in and sees that his daughter is to the left, on the front row, surrounded by her mother's family. He takes the first row on the right and is surprised to note that none of the rest have decided to join him here, not even his sister who was her best friend for almost all of the time he had known her himself. Now the minister is talking about her life, growing up and then her time with him and he turns his face away and the tears fall for the duration of this narrative. He turns to look at his daughter and she is stoic and resolute. She is solid too it seems. Outside they hug and he commends her on how held together she is. She starts to order him about, well in her way: "Will you do this, Dad? Will you get that, Dad?" So, now they are back to the level plane of the pendulum.

"Are you coming back to mine for a bit?"

"Yes, okay," he says. "Just for a while."

(Road Rage – Catatonia) 2 082 835

Brian clicked down the receiver and sat for a moment before moving into the hallway and picking a thick A4 envelope off the table. He ripped it open to reveal a glossy looking brochure full of images from a world of wildlife and a letter neatly folded and type-written at the back. He took the brochure and the letter and dropped them onto his dining table and made himself a cup of tea before reading the content. He knew it wouldn't be long before she called, and he wanted to be armed with as much information as he could before the call. He had to admit, he could see why his brother was so successful in business when faced with the power of his persuasion. The call came less than an hour later and as he suspected the turbulence in her tone suggested she hadn't read the letter.

"He's bought her a cell phone, Dad! A cell, you know my feelings and she's too young anyway and…"

"Amy! Stop! Have you read the letter?"

"What? What letter are you talking about?"

"The letter that came with the brochure?" There was a silence. "You haven't opened the brochure and seen the letter, have you?"

"He's bought her a cell phone! That is all I have seen and that is enough… She's not even old enough to know how to use it!"

"Amy? On her birthday what did she ask him for?" There was more silence. "Okay, clearly, he can't just pluck a penguin from off the world's surface! So, he adopted her a colony of them!"

"What has that got to do with a cell phone?" She screeched.

"From what I can gather my love, and you know me and technology, the cell he has sent her is linked to a satellite that can view the colony…"

"She has… The cell…" Brian laughed bemused.

"Yeah, I know. What's more, there are a group of scientists at a station in the Antarctic studying this colony and the cell phone is also linked to their observations... So apparently, she can view them at human contact level through the cell he has sent. He couldn't get her a penguin, so he got her everything within his power to get her a penguin!"

"Oh!"

"Read the brochure. From what I can gather he has also adopted her a herd of Elephants, a white rhinoceros, and a family of gorillas and that is as far as I have got!"

"What is he doing, Dad?"

"I think he is trying to help in the only way he can my love. All of his life he has been able to make money. I think somewhere along the way he had forgotten what he was making it for. I think he may have re-discovered, in his own mind, that purpose."

"Dad!? He can't just buy..."

"I think he knows that too, Amy, he called me before you did to try to explain to you that that is not what he is doing. He said he had never really helped anyone in his life before... Then he hung up. She has lit him up, my love, let us let him try and help, okay? Are you there Amy?"

"He gets one chance Dad. One! And anything else he wants to do for Jessica he comes through me first, okay Dad?"

"You got it kid!" Brian sighed heavily and back at the table smiled at the memory of his older brother paying a gang of jocks to do a number on another footballer who was bullying his kid brother in high school. Brian sipped his tea and said out loud: "You helped me once Brother. You helped me once!"

(Love of Strings – Moby) 6 953 110

It took several days' travel to reach their destination before the horse and cart his mother had bought veered down a track towards a thatched stone cottage overlooked by a steep hill. The Sun was rising above the hill and bright shafts of light fell upon the valley of their home through the branches of a large tree that stood at the apex of the hill, alone. Autumn was almost at an end and the morning chill that gripped him like a dry presence, like the tingling sting of the nettle, was suddenly warmed by the horses Tobias spotted grazing near the house. He turned to his mother who had followed her son's gaze and she nodded: "The white one is yours."

Tobias leapt off the cart and sprinted towards the equine beauty, a beast of shock white, that his mother had said belonged to him. He slowed as he got closer and stooped without stopping to tear thick clumps of grass in either hand as the horses eyeballed the approaching stranger warily and fussed, but only ever so slightly. "Easy there my beauties… Easy!" He said flattening out his hands and offering them the fresh grass he had picked. They fed hungrily as he stroked the warm, sharply defined muzzles, whispering his adulations of the magnificent beasts. His mother stopped outside the house some moments later and called for him.

"Come, Tobias. There is plenty of time to become acquainted!"

Tobias moved to the side of his great white horse and ran his hands over the strong, muscular body. "What am I to call you, my friend?" He whispered in the horse's ear. He thought of how fast he would be… Charge? Arrow? But immediately found himself thinking of the unfortunate King that had gone off too fast and was hacked to pieces in front of his eyes. His colour… Blizzard? No, too cold and calamitous. Then he thought of the other General, the one who watched as the King fell. The one on the white horse that seemed to move his whole army without moving a muscle, like magic! Magic! MAGIC! The horse neither agreed nor disagreed, just remained motionless. Tobias began to move towards the house thinking of his horse and the name he had just given him. No! No… "Merlin," he whispered, and the name clicked. "MERLIN!" He called out, turning to his horse who had looked back over his shoulder straight into the eyes of the excited boy. "Merlin!" He shouted in the valley and entered the door of his new home.

(Age of Magic – Trevor Jones) 29 391

The drinks flowed freely and so did the conversation. Jan and Sara were making themselves very acquainted, to the point of almost sitting in each other's space. Nicholas looked over to his new friend who looked back and slammed a hand on the table and shouted, loudly and drunkenly: "My friend!" Before looking around for Anke.

"Anke, more drinks my lady." Nicholas shook his head and re-focused his eyes, thinking: 'If Father could see me now!'

Arabella dropped her hand on his forearm, which startled him slightly: "Too much, English man!?" She laughed.

"Sorry, I was far away for a moment." Arabella removed her hand.

"You have a woman back in England, Nicholas?"

"No, no, nothing like that. I was thinking about my father. If he could see me. What brimstone would fall from his tongue!" Arabella removed her blue and yellow turban from her head and shook a full head of flaxen hair that danced upon her shoulders causing the nearby patrons to stop and watch the young woman place her elbows on the table, drop her chin into her cupped hands and face Nicholas: "Would your father resent so much his son having… err amusement, yah?"

"Chirping-merry is not a word foremost in my father's vocabulary, my dear Arabella, and I am extremely chirping-merry…" Arabella sat back in her chair and picked up her cup swinging it towards Nicholas smiling: "Nicholas! I too am very... Chirping-merry" And they clinked cups together as Anke returned to pour them more. A troupe of men began to dance in the centre of the Tavern as the chorus in the corner began a new song. Nicholas and Jan turned to watch, clinking their cups together, as the men before them danced. One of the group turned and ushered the cross-giver by the door to join them, who smilingly dismissed them animatedly with his hands before finishing his drink, crossed himself and joined the men who began clapping at the arrival of the old man. Nicholas laughed and picked up his stick banging the tip of it on the floor with approval. Jan moved closer to Nicholas and ushered for him to move in closer.

"Nicholas, Lady Sara has kindly volunteered to audience my work!" Nicholas looked at Jan perplexed. "She is coming back to my studio to view my art. Would you mind terribly?" Nicholas, a young man of confidence, fearless in most pursuits, suddenly looked panic stricken: "You're leaving?"

"Yes, my friend, we are leaving. You are not alone; you have Miss Arabella." Nicholas' eyes dropped and Jan laughed. "What is the matter my English friend? You never spoke to a woman alone before?" Nicholas said nothing and the smile left his face. All his life he had been confident. Speaking in crowds, with people, in any situation had never phased him. He grew up watching his father give speech after speech, sermon after sermon and his father had told him something that had stuck.

"When you are speaking to a crowd," he said. "Do not focus on the crowd! Instead, pretend you are talking to just one person. A person who holds your love, who has your respect. Do that and you may just charm the World my boy." The boy of then asked his father: "Who is your person father?" His father smiled and placed his hand on the Bible. The man of now wanted to ask his father: "What if confronted by potentially that person, right now, in person, face to face? What then Old Man?" In his head his father laughed and walked away: "You're a Man now my boy. You are a Man now!" Jan raised himself up and turned to Sara who had just finished her huddle with Arabella who looked gravely at Nicholas who shrugged his shoulders.

"Are you ready my dear? I have rivers and streams and trees and flowers at your disposal." Sara kissed her friend and joined Jan who leaned down and whispered into his friend's ear: "Remember, my friend, swans love water. They love the water!" Nicholas had no idea what Jan meant as he led lady Sara out of the door.

(Birdhouse in Your Soul – They Might Be Giants) 6 134 200

Chapter Twenty-one
What is it to be real? Some would say to be truthful.

Is that entirely true when the truth of your own reality may differ from the beneficiary of your own such wise and sage truth? There is only one truth and that is the truth you hold within you because that is your own reality. To be real is to be present and aware, conscious of the moment. Every precious breath, every breathtaking view, every forward step, every sliding minute. So many seconds, minutes, and hours we lose thinking of the next step while we are in the process of one already. So much of life wished away. Embrace the moment and sometimes the truth of it will be painful and other times it will be wonderful. Does the real me tell my mother, so small in my embrace. It is Christmas and I hug her, and she feels so small and frail, do I tell her that? Knowing in my heart she is anything but, even now. I remember watching her sprint from our home, pulling the slip-ons from her feet, as the older boy who had just punched her son in the face, fled as if escaping from wildfire, fear painted like a landscape in his young eyes. The woman who took his hand at his lowest of moments and said: "I wish I could do it for you, son, I wish I could because I would."

And the man of a hundred years later looked through the mists of his eyes and knew that she would and would do a hell of a better job of it.

"I know you would Mam!"

The truth isn't always as cut and dried as a simple phrase that can clumsily drop and roll from a careless tongue. Yes, she is small because I am bigger. Yes, she is frailer because the marching band of time doesn't stop – for any of us, yet. Would she still turn into a rampaging boulder of destruction if any of her offspring were threatened or in danger? Fuck yeah. That's the truth, I know it, she knows it, nothing needs to be expressed because that is a shared reality. Does he tell his children, as he runs his hands through their hair, that he feels like a soft wind embracing the flourishing forest leaves? That he will blow away anything that comes near to harm them? That he will blow the seeds of their ideas and their hopes and dreams and do everything in his power to make them flourish too? Maybe he should, maybe he should! Does he also tell them that often times he feels just like a child himself and that sometimes it is their light that guides him? He tells them that he loves them at every opportunity, at the end of every cinematic reel he spends with his children. That is real. That is truth. That is all they need to know! (The Man takes his mobile phone and texts his mother and his children: "I love you." Within minutes his family return the message, his mother even adds a new word to his vocab: Unizillions. And that is embracing the present…)

(Angels We Have Heard – Lindsey Stirling) 2 555 019

The Man sits at a breakfast table of the large dining area of the Cretan hotel. It isn't late though he has been up for hours, and the holiday makers are still filing in in drips and drabs. Last call for breakfast. It is getting on for 9am and he takes a sip of his fourth coffee of the day. It isn't greed, it is good coffee, and the cups are half mug size. A thick glass stands alone rinsed of the brace of apple juices he has chugged, and he begins cracking one of the boiled eggs he has in front of him. It has a face drawn on it… He doesn't remember the reason why now! He has already polished off the bacon, fried eggs, and beans with a couple of fresh bread buns. He doesn't do the sausages. Europe can't do sausages. Not the way the English do at any rate. A stack of pancakes sits in the middle of the table smothered in glistening golden syrup. He's tried the crepes, but they were flavourless, the French don't always get it right, so he's opted for the American. He doesn't think he will be able to finish all of them though, especially after the boiled eggs – he ain't Cool Hand Luke! He pulls off the mouth of the egg to reveal the shiny white meat within as he watches the families get served their breakfast and ruminates on the fact that it is his penultimate day here. After that, I'll do that, swim here, got a few hours before pick-up. Then he stops. He is already at the airport, for fuck's sake he is almost home, touchdown. He can feel the chill English Autumn wind on his summer skin. Stop! Look around. The Polish Lovers walk by and say hi, he returns the salutation and watches them as they make the long walk to the serving area, continuing to shell his egg. Look how slowly they walk. Look how they amble, as if time is in their hands. The clock ticks, but slower, his breathing deeper and more relaxed. What is the rush? The Sun is up – he knows that he went to greet it this morning with the steady swishing sound of the Sea lapping the beach on his left side – and it is warm, so wonderfully warm for an October morning. People, holiday makers, vacationers, chat idly. No stress, no mess, no bosses to impress! You'll be at work soon enough. Enjoy the moment. Feel the moment. Forget the past. Ignore the future. Live here, now. He polishes off the first egg and cracks the second. He is almost full, and he still has a plate of delicious pancakes to attempt. Coffee on tap. Fruit juice on tap. All the time in the world to enjoy. Eventually, he gets up to leave, on noticing the old Dutch man with the bad legs sat at his usual spot outside, he makes his way to the coffee machine and pours one – black no sugar. He strolls to the exit and approaches the man: "I'm leaving," he says as he drops the coffee in front of the grateful Dutch man. "Thank you, my friend," he says as the Man saunters over the bridge of the pool.

(Wonderful Life [Fairhide Mix] – Black) 56 122

Robert lost his father and lost his mind. Sometimes he thought he was a future self, caught in a past, totally unaware of his present. Strangers seemingly aware of him that he had no knowledge or recollection of would approach and he would stare blankly into their faces, like he was the face of a clock. He read and the information learnt, eddied in his mind, like a whirlpool dragging in fragments of other information to join the crazy swirling equations of his mind. Diagram after diagram littered the floor at his feet in the workshop, he was supposed to be repairing watches from. Words, pictures, all within the encompassing circle of a watch face he drew on every piece of paper he scrawled on. One such circle was half covered black, with a shiny orb within it, apparently representing the moon. The other half in flame orange, with a black ball at its centre representing the Sun. He began charting the sun's motion through the sky from his window drawing arcs and lines within the diagrams. One circle, dissected by a line, had the words

'Hour Rise Up.' Then the 'Up' scribbled out and replaced with 'On.' Rise on. Hour Rise On. Bracketed underneath the little phrase: Horus Eyes On, signifying the light of the Sun dawning a new day, lighting up the World in view. At the top of the circle, he wrote 'Solis' with arrows from the word to the dissecting line. On the other side of the line, he scrawled the lines: 'Sol Lays Here.' (The phrase seemed familiar to him, some Mythology he had read. Solaziar? Solacier? Solacia! Salacia!) He began by watching the Sun, in its crawl across the sky from his window, hand on his chest measuring the beat of his heart and drawing dots within the encompassing circle. When this endeavour frustrated him, he began climbing upon the roof of his building, a piece of slate and chalk within his grasp. He began charting the first semblance of light, hand on heart, dotting inside the circle which he had drew upon the slate. When the traders below got so noisy, he could barely hear himself he would accompany this procedure with a consistent and droning 'Tick.' Tick. Tick. Tick. Sometimes he would do this for the entire day and right through the night. Never stopping to eat, sleep or even piss. Newcomers to the street would point and ask. The traders would reply with 'Robert Solace.' The night drunks, falling around the plagued London Street would laugh, gin bottle to their lips and point at the man perched upon his roof watching the Moon: 'LunaTick Bob! LunaTick Bob!'

When he wasn't on the roof, he was drawing diagrams and counting dots or writing something or other scrawled on small pieces of paper. 'Ghosts they come and ghosts they go they pull my clothe and mess my hair but when I turn there be not there!' When he finally slept, he slept for days at a time. Always around 3 days. 72 hours.

(Time [Cyberdesign] – Hans Zimmer) 21 941

A greying Epsilon began the ascent of the great tree, his children in tow, his mate was at the foot of the tree hooting as the young male and female followed their father branch for branch. Epsilon turned for a long second and fixed a stare at his mate. She slapped the trunk of the tree and fist punched the floor and threw leaves into the air. He sighed and carried on as the first warm fingers of sunlight appeared. He moved with speed and agility through the middle of the branches of the tree, every so often, for only seconds, stopping to see if his children were still behind him. They were. Through the middle and on and on. He looked back and saw the apprehension in the wide eyes of the young apes who strove on determinedly anyway. Three quarters up and the sumptuous fruit appeared, such colour, such richness, but Epsilon carried on regardless. On and on. His children had stopped. He hooted and they hooted back up at him as they picked and began biting into the bounty they had come across. His hooting got louder but they threw away their fruit and began playing among the branches above the canopy of most of the other trees in the forest. Epsilon lowered his hand to descend and then looked up and carried on with more speed. They had no necessity to scale the height of the great tree, not the one he had had so many years before and without realising it tears fell from the big brown orbs of the aging ape as he instinctively piloted the ascent. His head broke through the canopy as the dazzling ball of orange appeared on the horizon causing him to close his eyes as the warmth hit his face. If apes could smile, he was smiling. He could hear the playful chirps of his children down below and with just his head above the top of the tree he quickly began his descent. Quicker now. Within seconds he was at the level of his children and began chasing them around the branches of the tree as they grunted excitedly, moving downwards, spiralling the great tree towards the forest floor. They were so fast and agile, faster than he ever was. When they reached the bottom, they ran and jumped into the arms of their waiting mother who patted and smothered them before they ran off to play. Epsilon negotiated the last couple of branches cautiously as his mate fixed him with a stare. If apes could look sternly, she looked sternly at him now. If eyes could say: 'You ever... And I'll fuckin kill you!' That was her eyes, and he knew, and he dropped from the tree and lowered himself, his eyes looking up at her. She fixed, then released and Epsilon moved around behind his mate and snuggled in, dropping his big ape arms over her shoulders.

(Children – Robert Miles) 989 922

What began as a telephone conversation that started with the phrase: "I have an idea!" quickly snowballed into something none of them expected. Uncle A, as he now preferred to be termed by the little girl that had won his heart, had offered a large cash incentive for anyone that could offer his great niece a lifeline and he spent just as much advertising the fact. It didn't matter how long the line was, no-one appeared to be a match. Sometimes he wondered whether God himself was reviled by the idea that a mere mortal could succeed where he had failed. He wouldn't give up, he never had, and he certainly wouldn't stop on the most important client in his life.

He now saw her every few days, always with permission from her mother who never left her daughter's side, the rings around her eyes testimony to the fact that some things are more important than sleep. At first, he would visit in his lunch hour, which he used to take at his desk. Now he spent more and more time away from the office, a move that surprised many there, not least the manager that now had the pleasure of being delegated more responsibility, more personal culpability and far less scrutiny from the omnipresence of what many would have termed workaholic. Adam Cathcart was a changed man and the change affected everyone around him for the better. One employer had even started referring to him as 'Scrooge with Soul.' Never to his face of course, not if they ever wanted to work in business again, and a little unfairly because he wasn't actually a miser – just a man that had nothing he didn't already want and nobody else to spend it on. That changed. Jessica loved her gift from him, and the cell phone and her colony of penguins were never far away from her side. She'd even named them all and told him one day: "That one, look, that one I have called Uncle A, like you…"

He'd watched as the penguin marched around the colony and then would stop and dip its beaked head into its chest against the Arctic wind.

"Why that one?" He had asked.

"Because it is on its own!" He had chuckled, but the words had pricked and hurt him inside like the Arctic wind. He couldn't help but feel a small tug of sadness at the fact, though it didn't show and maybe didn't show until later that night when he would involuntarily find himself thinking about Rosa and where and what she might be doing now.

(Gift of a Thistle – James Horner) 1 526 949

Tobias soon discovered that the truth of owning and riding a fine stallion was that the first lesson was to learn how to fall. Soon, he learned how to fall without hurting himself. Not long after that he learned how to fall with grace. Eventually, the true lesson hit home. He wasn't riding a machine, but a fine animal of flesh and bone and sinew and heart and spirit. How could he expect to impose his own will on such a splendid creature without the awareness of such a simple and fundamental truth? Let him run, let him run free, and ride the muscles of his body like a fast-flowing wave. The rain cascaded down as the boy gripped tightly to the animal beneath him charging to the top of the hill that overlooked his cottage in the valley. By the time they reached the top, the rain had stopped: "Woah! Woah boy!" They strode, calmly, man and horse at the top of the hill, as one, ambling around the old oak tree that stood there. They stopped and looked at the glorious vista before them. Then Tobias squeezed in his heels and commanded: "Go, Merlin! Go." And they bolted, oh so fast, down the gradient of the steep hill towards home.

(Boadicea – Enya) 12 928 473

It was while visiting that his idea had taken root, grew legs, and ran the four-minute mile and then ran round again to do a lap of honour. Jessica had just called his brother Grandad B, to which Adam had put his hand to his mouth and asked to be excused, stifling breaking into hysterical laughter, as his younger brother looked open mouthed from the widely gaping smile of his granddaughter to the perpetrator of the in-joke between the brothers that only one of them found funny. Even Amy looked away, trying not to laugh. Adam returned and Brian eyeballed him: "You're an asshole!" Adam had laughed as he sat back down.

"I'm sorry Brian, I couldn't resist," he said, as he fixated on one of the colourings pinned up above Jessica's bed. The picture displayed a pulsing bright orange and red sun seemingly drinking from the azure blue of the sea it was rising up over. Orange and red sparkles glittered towards the artist perspective and dark craggy rocks to the right of the picture hung across in dark shadow. It reminded him… He stood and leaned in towards the picture.

"This picture? Jessica? Have you been here?" Jessica, sat cross-legged upon her hospital bed, looked up and Amy remarked: "She's never been here Adam. She's never seen the sea… Well, when she was a few months old but apart…" Jessica finger in mouth called out.

"My dream picture." She said. "Yes, my dream picture!" Adam looked at her mother and in incredulous tones remarked: "This picture could be my morning view. A bloody replica!" Amy shrugged her shoulders: "Well, what do you know!"

"No, seriously, Amy!" Jessica bounced excitedly on the bed: "Can I see it? Can I see it Uncle A?"

"Jessica, no…" Amy had said tiredly. But Adam had wondered then and as he left and then later and for days after.

"Why can't she?"

(Blue, The Colour of Dreams – Yakuro) 844 182

Brian Cathcart awoke from a deep and delicious sleep to the telephone ringing. At first, he was going to ignore it and drift back away and then his eyes opened widely, and he was fully awake: "Jessica!"

He moved quickly and picked up the receiver and nervously: "Hello…" The other voice on the end of the phone was also excited but in a different way.

"Brian? I have an idea!" Brian let out a full body of breath and whispered.

"Thank God!"

"What?"

"Never mind… What do you want Adam?"

"I have an idea. Please, hear me out!" He knew then he was about to listen to hard sell Adam go to work and by the time he had clicked down the receiver he wondered what he had just agreed to. He convinced himself it wasn't all one-sided. He had made sure, stressed the fact, that Amy would be consulted every step of the way should he fight his corner on the issue. Adam, a man that was used to doing everything his own way admitted that the concession would be difficult for him but concede he absolutely would to whatever demand she would put in place.

(Stand by Me – Oasis) 109 568 744

The specialist was furious and paced the ward like a key-turned toy: "This is most irregular! Most irregular indeed!" Adam stood unperturbed as Amy tried to placate the excited little man apologetically. Like all things Adam had conducted proceedings like they were a business transaction.

"Mrs Simpson. No… Just no. This just isn't right! It is not right…" The specialist was saying, and Adam saw the blood rise to his nieces face and stepped in, taking the man aside by the arm. Brian also moved over to where the two men huddled as Amy took hold of a fully clothed Jessica in her arms. Adam began in hushed tones.

"I think you will find this is happening, with or without your consent. The Board was unanimous in its decision. If you have an issue, please take it up with them. While you are at it explain to them the measures you have in place to substitute the very generous donation from a local businessman that will finance the construction of a new wing."

(Gathering the Clans – Braveheart) 52 254

Brian pushed his brother aside with the back of his hand before the confrontation became any more vehement.

"Dr Shaw, please see it from our point of view. If, God forbid, we can't get her a donor, what quality of life does she have left?"

The doctor sat: "She needs constant and consistent care. Consistent. Medicines…"

"And she will have it, I promise you sir. No detail will be overlooked. Believe me, we would rather have you on side than against us." The little man looked defeated and exasperated as Brian began to walk away.

"Love will not cure your granddaughter Mr Cathcart!"

Brian stopped and the bones in his cheeks tensed as he turned on the little man who seemed to shrink in his chair.

"Maybe not, that maybe true DOCTOR! But it will go a hell of a lot further than your objective weekly visits or array of pills… I think we may have to reconsider the specialist that presides over the care of my grand-daughter!" Brian stressed angrily. "Have a nice day sir!"

(For the Love of a Princess – Braveheart) 1 370 271

Adam stood by the window overlooking the tranquil lapping of waves on the dark Ocean view before him. The Moon sent glittering parcels of light upon its surface. Cell phone to his ear. He felt a serenity, a calmness that always followed the flowering of an idea that blossomed and grew. An idea he would make work. He had frantically moved through the rooms of his palatial home just hours before, imagining the set-up and building it up in his mind.

"I have an idea!" He was in pitch mode. "Why don't they move in here?"

"Adam…What are you talking about? She is in hospital, she is ill, she needs care, she needs to be in HOS-PIT-AL! Do I need to spell it out? I'm not sure your seaside Xanadu is exactly the place for her, do you?"

"Please, hear me out!" For the next hour Brian Cathcart wrestled with the twists and turns of his elder brother's arguments and despite the soft tones and into-nations felt as if he had been in a fight by the end of the conversation; a fight he didn't know whether he had won or lost. In the end, their own personal estrangement needed to be put aside for the good, for the wellbeing of his family, and he decided Adam had sold that part at least. Adam walked away from the window and sat at his desk working out the details of how he could bring his idea to fruition. There would be much resistance. He Googled 'St John's Hospital' and looked to see who was on the Board. As the first spears of light gathered on the horizon, he had already converted his home in his mind and began writing his proposal.

(Xanadu – Olivia Newton-John) 13 466 454

Chapter Twenty-two

We build, every day building. Homes, and shops, and malls, and businesses, and hospitals, and parks, and statues, and, in antiquity, mystical monoliths, and spaces of mythological projection and theory.

We are all building and creating, creating with every word, every action, building up relationships. Building up connections. Building up our hearts, minds and spirits to hopefully something wonderful and beautiful for ourselves and for those we love and for the World around us. Do we always get it right first time? I'm sure we don't all of the time and you only need to look at the art of any creation to see that. How many layers of paint, how much fabric, has gone into the masterpiece we idly and subjectively saunter by in the gallery? How many drafts of lyrics and different melodies and beats does the performing artist go through before landing on the song and tune that sweetly dances in the conch of our ears. Sometimes maybe, we build that house of straw the wolf so easily blows down before realising that what is required is solid and steadfast. A home that keeps out the spectre of the carnivorous wolf so maligned by fairy-tale. We may even be building all the components of that steadfast home, that crux of security, without first laying the foundations the house will sit upon. The house without foundations! Does it flounder and fall in Mother Nature's breath, rolling across her skin like a tumbleweed? Or does it float and fly into a world of imagination that only the dreamer can perceive? I don't know, maybe it is better to take hold of the spade and dig those foundations deep. Deep enough for that home to sit securely enough to house the dreamer and their imaginings in a space of security. Or perhaps, like the long-living tortoise and turtle, home is where they drop down, come wind, rain or shine. Or like the dreamer, home is where their imaginings take them.

(Le Vent, Le Cri [Figure Skating] – Ennio Morricone)
68 681

Most of the Tavern had dispersed once the corner choir had finally finished its serenade and Arabella leaned in: "Tell me about your father Nicholas."

"My Father?"

"Yah, he seems very important to you!"

"Is that strange? Shouldn't he be?"

"Of course, as is mine." Nicholas thought for a moment.

"The short version!" He cleared his throat. "Poor man, sold leather in the dirty streets, to pious Parliamentarian powerhouse parodied by his peers!"

Arabella laughed. "Did you write that?"

Nicholas smiled. "He built a powerful life for himself, for me, a life I am grateful for, with a book and an unshakeable faith in the power of God and Jesus Christ. I don't know whether there is much more I can say…"

"But what was he like as a faa-ther?" Nicholas squinted his eyes at the interrogation. "Loving, Arabella…" He looked straight into her. "Loving, but preoccupied. Protective but with a demand for one's own belligerence." He took a gulp of ale. "Pretty soon I became more protective of him. I watched as his political peers threw him from the fortifications into a moat of obscurity and he barely… Not a flicker of vengeance upon his countenance!" Arabella took his left hand. "But me…" He rapped a fisted right hand on his chest. "I felt it, Arabella. I felt it in here. In my gut, in my stomach, in my heart, like a fire raging. I was a boy, but I didn't need protecting!" He looked at the beauty across the table. "I'm sorry, I…"

"It's fine."

"My father is, in his heart, a peaceful man… He taught me that we all have to find that in our own way. Some find it easier than others." She pulled her hand back and folded her arms in front of her on the table.

"My father was a war hero and is a successful trader. He could marry me off to a good family if he so wished. But from an age I can remember he always said that he would rather have a happy daughter than an influential son in law." She smiled serenely.

"That's a beautiful sentiment," Nicholas said quietly.

"He sometimes jests that both would be good! But he supports me, and I support him. As you do your father, and your father does you." Nicholas nodded. Arabella sat upright. "It is getting late; I should be getting home."

"I will walk you!"

"There is really no need." She said reapplying her silken turban.

"I insist." Nicholas stated, picking up his stick and squaring the bill.

(Son of a Preacher Man - Dusty Springfield) 20 509 479

It was Carl Simpson that had been the most difficult to convince. It took every acreage of his wives subtle and sincere tenderness that she believed this was the right thing for them to do to convince him. Sometimes, the man, enclosed in the prickly privets of his own pride, finds it hard to look over the hedge and see the green pastures beyond. He was a working man and a working man he was. He paid. He provided. It was his duty. "It's your duty to be there for your daughter… No hospital bills to pay, Carl, means less hours at work means more time with me and Jess!" She had taken to the privet with a chainsaw and inch by inch it was coming down. Adam offered him a job, he refused. Construction was all he had done. "So, help with the building of your part of the house then!" Adam had blasted. "I will," Carl had retorted. "When I finish work…" And so it was. That was how Carl agreed on his own terms. Adam had glanced at Amy, who nodded ever so slightly, and walked away calling Carl a stubborn young man. He smiled inside, they had both won.

(Ride A White Swan – T Rex) 243 207

His father whispered in his ear: "Capture the Minotaur, Robert! Capture the Minotaur!" He awoke with a start and sat, bolt upright in his bed, his shadow dancing on the wall in the candlelight. "What? What do you mean Father?" He rubbed his eyes and looked around the room, for a figure that wasn't there. "The Minotaur?" He had read of the Gods and the exploits of their heroic sons and immediately reran the story of Theseus through his head, looking for some clue as to what it could possibly mean. Theseus, who had bravely offered himself as a sacrifice in order to defeat the cruel beast. He had required help, help from... Ariadne! She had known the secrets of the labyrinth. But he knew of no such person in his own life that could help him in whatever undertaking it was he was being asked. She had given him string. Rope. Thread. A ball of string so that he could find his way back out of the maze should his endeavour succeed, and the Minotaur be slain. He invested in a ball of twine and played and fiddled with it as if he were kitten. He unravelled the string, constantly, throwing it around his workshop. He held it aloft and watched as it unwound and then he would wind it back up and repeat the process. He drew sketches. That again, lay carelessly at his feet. "What are you asking of me Father?" He despaired. "And what of the Minotaur?" He awoke again with a start later that night.

"Capture the mine-yoot-hour! Robert!"

(Shadows – Lindsey Stirling) 158 948 364

The Man has been wondering for weeks whether he should include this section and if so, to what extent does he involve the other person. This writing, this project, this whatever it may be, is not and has never sought to be a character assassination and yet a building, a progress of fibre, involves, usually the expertise of an artisan of some description. A plumber, joiner, electrician rarely fall into the hands of just one – unless they are polypractical of course! The Man, though stand alone and more so at this moment in time that at any time in his life, knows that his structure, his views, on life, on love, are coloured (and on the whole beautifully coloured, kaleidoscopically, he has to admit!) by the other person he shared his life and of course his love with. Sometimes the Man, any man, maybe women as well, will leave a relationship, split up, whatever and not accept their part in the ultimate demise of it. As if, in collecting their belongings, bags, cases, CD's, all the assortment, there includes a big bag of sand with a small hole in it. That sand is their share of the blame for the breakdown and like the top-heavy cone of the hourglass, full, but slowly leaking in the gentle passing of time remembers only from the passive-victim mentality of it and not the many reasons they were there in the first place or their own active part in the breakdown. There is character and there is circumstance. Sometimes the two cannot be consolidated. The Man, his bag of sand empty, searches within the hemp sack to realise the crunching beneath his feet, within his shoes, is the sand he conveniently forgot to remember for so long.

(For Love One Can Die [Figure Skating] – Ennio Morricone) 4 391 881

Chapter Twenty-three
I used to think I was good at relationships, but when you excavate the bones.

The relationships, those of intimacy, in my own case between a man and woman, because that is my own personal aesthetic, teach us so much about ourselves. Possibly lessons we don't realise we are learning while sailing along on the tranquil rivers of their existence. Maybe we don't even learn them when the currents of the river turn against the little boat and hamper its progress. Little waves crashing against the side, then bigger waves lapping over the side of it. That is when the Captain, the skipper of the little vessel, realises that they have to fight on against the current or turn the boat around, change direction, look for the more tranquil waters. The easier more peaceful navigable route. Is love supposed to be so difficult? The skipper of this particular boat doesn't think so because he believed it came easy to him! Not the girls, that had never been easy, well, sometimes, sometimes not. Was it all just words? Was it all just words? Hot air from bloodless blue lips and an empty damp rock of a heart? No! He is being unfair to himself and, as he thinks, deep diving for the emotional memory, he knows that. Was it ever that easy? No! He knows that too. Did he ever love? Yes, he did. He loved and left, he loved and lost, he loved and tries to forget, he loved…

(i) There was a girl, the year is 1992…
(ii) There was a girl, the year is 1996…
(iii) There was a girl, the year is 2002…
(iv) There was a girl, the year is 2003…

(The Power of Love – Frankie Goes to Hollywood) 3
343 811

Between writing section (i) and section (ii) which I was going to do until falling asleep, I had a dream, a dream I have just woken from and writing it now while it is fresh. I was laid on my front in the grass. Short grass, like a football field. The whole scenario reminded me a little of when you were young and were watching a sports day at school. I was minding my own business when a woman and two girls – I say girls, they were late teens/early twenties and one of them I had the feeling I had already seen before arriving at this spot on the grass. She teased me then, like she teases him now, in the dream. She picks up a hand-full of grass and sprinkles it over his head. He ignores her, though he is acutely aware using peripheral vision which one it is. The woman moves away, not angrily but in a way that suggests 'she is at it again' kind of attitude. I think she is a relative, but not necessarily her mother. She is laughing and is energetic. She does it again and this time he looks then looks away. Then she sprinkles the grass over him, but with dirt or dust and twigs and grass, like you do sometimes when pulling from the loosened surface of vegetation, and she lays down next to him laughing. He laughs back saying: "What are you doing?"

But he puts his head over her body and shakes the contents of what she has laced his hair with back onto her with his hand. She has dark hair, and enormous dark eyes with freckles on her cheek and across her nose. Her features are big, or seem big, but she is not big in figure. Her features are prominent. Big eyes, strong face and mouth. She was to the left of him and now to the right sitting up and saying: "Four in a bed!" He has sat up. The others have said: "Don't include us. It's you who wants to cuddle or fuck!" I get aroused because her smile is clearly coming on to me and she says: "What do you want to do?" This time, she is not teasing, and they go off together. "Where are we going to go?" He asks and they enter a building and he/I move her against a wall and pull down her face mask and we kiss tenderly, teasing, before a passionate kiss ensues and when he looks again, he sees for the first time she is wearing an eye-patch, but he has no idea whether it is through an aesthetic choice or necessity. He touches it softly with his hand and still can't determine. She takes his hand, and they head off, somewhere... Then I awake. What was her name? The first name he recognised as belonging to her, the only name that came into his mind, was Daisy.

(Return to Innocence – Enigma) 118 919 106

There was a girl, the year is 1992 and the Man is a young man who, just six weeks before, had lost four of his best friends in a car accident which had killed them all instantly. He is looking down at his best friend sat and crying on the step to the function room of the engagement celebration he has stepped away from to share in the grief. They should have been here. All of them, especially Micky, who he hadn't managed to have a conversation with about the scenario – and now he was dead, and the conversation would forever, in this lifetime at least, remain silent.

Pretty soon we settled into a life of non-marital bliss. We both had completely different views on this subject. Not long after the engagement she was designing her own wedding dresses, sketching them in an artist pad as we lay in bed and asking my opinion on such things. Her Arian impatience to get hitched a lesson in fear, my 18-year-old self had never yet experienced. I just wanted the engagement party! I hadn't with any consciousness looked beyond that. She'd show me her sketches and I probably remarked how lovely they were with the inner me saying 'chill out, I'm eighteen, with no intention of marrying in the near future!'

I think it was about 1988 when first I saw her. My virginal frame at once besotted and intimidated by the girl in my presence. Older, confident, seemingly popular, fit as in good at sports and fit in all the other ways too. Long dark, black hair, always immaculately presented, hair, make-up, spoke rapid and laughed freely and always to me as if she was some kind of older female relative looking out for me. That isn't strange I suppose, she was my dad's partner's sister and they already had one child and soon another would be on the way. This dynamic could get confusing! If we ever married, she would have been both auntie and sister-in-law to my half-siblings…

The boy moves through the house and stops in the kitchen, looking out of the window at her. She is beautiful and mature – like a woman, even though she is only a year older - and so vivacious. It is her sister's 21st and Dad is playing his guitar. The months, the years, roll by and she sets him up with one of her friends. She always asks with an inquisitive excitement how the relationship is going. Time passes. He is instrumental in setting her up with one of his best friends. One of the finest young men ever created, hard and soft, generous, and caring, loved by men and women alike. They go out. He is walking up the road with a young lady, they leave and go in the opposite direction. He is not a virgin anymore. That ship sailed some time ago and its addictive quality pumps in his blood.

"Let's fuck!" He says.

When has such a brutal statement ever worked? For fuck's sake. She takes his hand and leads him behind a high wall on the way up to her home… Sometime later he is in the kitchen of her house, it is late or early, whichever way you look at it, they are drinking, and she asks him: "What happened?"

"We were behind that wall; you know the one?" She nods smiling. "She takes me through the bushes. Just getting started, you know? Then her brother, must have been behind us, stops and has a piss on the other side of the bushes!"

"You're kidding!"

"I fucking kid you not, I actually stopped breathing!"

They start laughing… They start working at a holiday camp close to where his dad lives, four of them, his best friend an old friend re-acquainted at college (still friends) and his friend. We live in a small caravan behind a pub. It is July. They regularly go out, they are eighteen, working and awaiting the A Level results that could make or break their lives. That is how it feels at that age. She is out often too, she is single too, maybe very recently. There is a function on, in the same function room they would host their engagement party. Where is his best friend? The toilet? The bar? They are talking, close, and they kiss. Then he feels a hand grab the collar of his shirt from behind and he is being tossed aside. His best friend is angry, but he cannot ultimately stop the inevitable. Now. Now! NOW... He needs to have the conversation. He is off work and so is his best friend. He is laying on the bed and reading when the daughter, a friend to us all, of the landlord of the pub enters, grave faced...

There was a fatalism to this first love of his. Not because he can honestly say with any confidence that there was a straight up black and white lesson learned from it – even though he knows there were plenty of lessons he did learn. It was one night; they had been drinking and he was walking her home. One of his caravan friends had tagged along, the friend of his college friend, and he wondered why. He wanted to tell him to fuck off but he was a mate, so he held onto it. They reached her house, and he recalls she was going to just go in, without inviting them in, even though his friend seemed to think she was because he was about to head on down the path. Then it came, popped out, spewed out, sailed out, floated out, danced out, without his awareness or apparent participation, loud and assured: "I Love You!"

She stops at the front door and looks straight into him. His friend has stopped midway down the path looking shocked.

"Come on," she says and unlocks her front door. He strides up the path and past his friend: "Goodnight ____!" He says, turning, as he reaches the door and heads on inside. That is the beginning of their relationship.

(The Bitterest Pill – The Jam) 2 154 403

The 1992 Summer season at the holiday camp had come to an end and I waved goodbye to my friends as I remained in Yorkshire, living in the house my fiancé shared with her father. She was working at a local hairdresser and I secured a job at a local printing firm doing piecework, a job that offered little security, as the amount of hours and hence money earned depended on the amount of work available shared between six of us that scrambled like hungry seagulls to secure as much work for ourselves, out of the work available, as possible. As a result, the hours were often short and my fiancé nine times out of ten would arrive home from work later than myself. This was my first taste of a dynamic with a woman that demanded more than the cursory 'I'll see you later!' Or a living condition with females entirely different from that shared with siblings and one's mother. I had to listen! For the first time in my life, I had to feign interest in the emotional and practical wellbeing of a person other than myself and I didn't realise how difficult that could be, how taxing on one's own time and sovereignty. I soon learned an aspect of my character that would perhaps become thematic throughout my early relationships; I could get bored very easily! From passion to indifference in 0-60, like an emotional, emotionless Bugatti. If I remember rightly, and maybe I don't, there was always drama at her workplace. The girls she shared her working environment with were always picking on her, bullying her, and this always struck me as strange because of how strong and forthright she could be in other situations. So, I listened and offered my commiserations and then we would go out and I would see their interactions out of the workplace; the smiles, the hugs, and think what the fuck is she talking about? You have to remember I was barely an adult and had no conception of the sometimes manipulative and backstabbing behaviour of women who share spaces together, so her gripes quickly became blurs in my ears, vowels and consonants with no real substance or meaning. I was losing interest.

Nothing was ever too much for her on a secular level. She looked after me, really looked after me. Made sure my packed lunch was always brimming, cooked like a MasterChef. Birthdays, Valentines, made the most amazing meals. If ever a man needed a mother hen, he found one and as I write I know she has children and I'm sure, no certain, that she will be the most providential and attentive mother. The problem was… I didn't need a mother.

As Winter moved into Spring, we both began working at the holiday park for the upcoming season and though on the surface everything seemed okay I think by then we had hurt each other enough to know that it wasn't going to last. Her fiery passion with my, mostly, cold indifference led to the scenario that would break the back of the donkey, topple the trees. Some weeks into our employment she told me she had become infatuated with another man that worked at the holiday camp.

I was unnaturally cool and reserved on the issue. A man in the flames of love, on the shores of blissful endurance, any man, would have done something about this surely? I didn't. I respected that at times people become attracted to other people even in the throes of commitment, I respect it still, that she had the strength of character to tell me something like that. When she asked me if she could stay at his caravan overnight, I said that she could when every cell in my body screamed that she couldn't. I was soft, but I was still a man dammit! She went anyway and then less than 24 hours later I was gone too.

(Lost in the Shadows – The Lost Boys) 1 280 960

They keep in touch whilst he is attending the University of Wolverhampton. He has to admit he hates it here and longs for the company of those who know him. When she arrived home from her liaison the previous night, as the man lay on their bed thinking, pondering, wondering whether there was any other option, it appeared to him that what she discovered was not what she was expecting. The man had decided there absolutely was no other option and had packed up all his things and waited for her to arrive home. Her apparent devastation surprised him, possibly even more, and watching the mascara riddled lines run down her face opened up his own floodgates. It was awful. The love may have been still there, but for my part at least, the trust certainly wasn't. I stayed at Dads for a while before heading back home and then eventually to here.

University. In a shared house, with one guy who I really liked and two girls. First impressions! Funny thing, and my Subliminist mind wonders if there is something in it. Does that first impression decide? He terminated at the bus station in the centre of Wolves, checking the backside and legs of his jeans for any sign of dampness, for the anxiety, that of feeling like he had pissed himself, re-emerged like a great burning Trojan Horse whenever faced with a situation with even the slightest hint of trepidation. Satisfied, he was okay, drizabone, he alighted from the vehicle and introduced himself to his new housemates that had come to meet him. He picked up his case that sat at the kerbside and the handle snapped, clean off, his case dropped loudly to the floor and the completely embarrassed little boy, walked through the centre of Wolverhampton with a case clutched in both arms and sometimes balanced atop his head.

Some months in she came to visit him. He can still remember her impatience to disembark from the moving vehicle as he waited for her at the bus terminal. They hadn't seen each other for months and after a few days in her company he would only see her once more. He only saw her once more. Strange, considering the familial circumstance. His excitement at seeing her now and his sadness at seeing her leave was precipitated by a loneliness the man would experience at times throughout his life and had learned to live with? Does he love or does he hate the loneliness? Is it a light chasing the shadows away? He was miserable where he was in Wolverhampton and wanted to be amongst the throng of student life in Telford where his course was based and so a plan formulated in his childish brain. The halls of residence there were full – for single people. There were residential places available for married students. Had he been drinking? He can't remember. He stood in the phone box at the end of the street of his residence. He does remember, the nerves, the procrastination, picking up the phone and returning it to its cradle. Eventually, he did dial, and kismet kissed him on the forehead or punched him in the gut.

"Hello, ___! Is _____ there?"

"No, Lee, she's gone out."

And so, it was. Had she been there he would have asked and at that moment was certain she would have said yes. As another sunshine climbed the horizon so did another decision. "I'm leaving this place!" And all thoughts of marriage disintegrated like dry autumn leaves, rubbed, and dropping from his soft ex-student hands. She went on to marry her childhood sweetheart and have children, children I suspect adored and adoring of the passionate woman he once knew. He hopes with all sincerity and without condescension that she is happy. He truly does.

(Life for Rent – Dido) 64 537 413

There was a girl, the year is 1996. The ground is icy, and the wind is cold but not as brutal as the cutting North Sea wind experienced in the Northeast. He has moved to the Midlands, Coventry, following a request from his best friend to join him here. He was the manager in a betting shop, but he knew he was just charting time, walking the bubble of comfort, so the pitch his friend had made was good, persuasive, but he was ready for a new adventure anyway. "I've got an idea," he said and within a week or two the man had left his job and moved into a dinghy house with his friend and currently walking home from a night shift at a crisp factory. "If we budget," he was saying. "We'll be able to buy our first caravan in a few months. Rent it out. Use the proceeds to go to another one. Just keep building." He listened, he always trusted that his best friend would never be short financially. There is an astuteness of such matters he sees ingrained within him. If he were on board, neither would he, despite his own indifference to the bears and bulls of Capitalism. He is here because he misses his best friend and is ready to embark on a new journey, experience new things, let his Mam have a decent night's sleep!

Some would maybe have seen him, over the next few years, as cold and aloof while others would have seen him as reckless. He was neither and both of those things and all the grey in between. What a World, that we should define the complexity of a human with one or two adjectives! He had a whimsical determination, a contradiction in itself. Dichotomous hippopotamus. Without the weight or aggression without fear or suppression. By the year 1996 he had lost the pillar of his youth and then a year later four pillars of his early adulthood, saved up to travel around Europe – Bohemian style – only to arrive back on the shores, wind in his long hair, eyeing the chalk cliffs of home, three days later. Lived the peasant but artistic life without ever producing anything. Been to and left University, without ever really giving it a try. He was a doer without the effort. In a video he made he referred to this time, between the death of his friends and what was about to be, as the wilderness years. Looking back and feeling the lazy faith he had in himself, trying to find a foothold on something, anything, that wasn't quicksand, he thinks he sees it now. Many, many years later his mother expressed how he had changed after their death. He hadn't seen it, then. Yes, he sees it now.

Radiant, blue marbles smiled at him over a packing machine in the factory and whether he wanted to or not he smiled and smiled wide. She had that immediate effect. Like all her happiness radiated from her baby blues and wide smile. They kept arriving together at the machine from different lines and each time her smile was just the same. A guy, some team leader, supervisor or whatever had clearly seen the situation and told each of us, we found out later, that the other had told him that they wanted to go out on a date with them. This never happened but he convinced me at least. So, I told him to tell her to wait outside for me after work so we could arrange it, swap numbers. That morning as the sun hung in the icy blue sky, she was waiting outside of the doors for him, and his friend smiled and walked on: "Catch me up!" She was small, or seemed small he remembers, and had reddish brown hair and her eyes were lit up, brightly in the morning sun as bright as her smile. They were both off the following day, so they arranged to meet at a local pub in Town they both knew that evening. For the next year, she either shared the house he shared with his best friend or the bedsit she had inhabited for the past year. She was 18 years old.

(Killing Me Softly – The Fugees) 226 189 124

From the get-go, it was clear that she would be in his life for some time. It wasn't because it was a wave crashing against rocks kind of love; molten lava bursting from the open mouth of a volcano or the earth-moving rubbing of tectonic plates. Don't get me wrong, the raw and harsh spouts of jealousy within each of us would rear its ugly head at times, usually in drink, but on the whole, the relationship was peaceful, friendly. There was a care and tenderness here, a need to look after her rather than in the previous relationship where it was the other way around and she looked after him. She lived an independent lifestyle, but she was so young and naïve, or seemed it to him at any rate, so meek and sweet as if life could break her at any moment but that she faced with an optimism of spirit he hadn't really noticed in anyone before. Life had already broken her in some respects; she had lost her mother when she was young and had spent her secondary school years being bullied, but just got on with it. Didn't cry, didn't complain, kept on walking, through the rain. Women usually took to her innocent personable charm and the men that didn't want to sleep with her saw her like a little sister, as his best friend clearly did throughout their relationship, and those that did want to sleep with her probably felt a strong urge to protect her. Many saw her as meek and soft and harmless like a kitten. Sometimes the Man would remind these people that on the whole she was, but know this, and he would pull out his arm and show the arc of a scar tracing his elbow.

This was some years later, and they lived together in Middlesbrough by now. It was Christmas Eve, either 1998 or 99, but it was Christmas Eve because he had gone out and promised to be in between 8 and 9 to help her wrap their daughter's presents. When he didn't roll in until after midnight. Big mistake! She spat venom at him like a venomous snake and he replied, probably without the venom, but with the lazy indifference or skewed higher ground he could sometimes muster that pissed his partners off something chronic. "I've got you a parmo haven't I!" (Parmo, exclusive to Middlesbrough!) He was tucking into his own, on the front room side of the breakfast bar. He didn't see her until it was too late. He saw her charging towards him and the next he knew his elbow had gone through a window that backed onto an anteroom of the property they rented. The whole window smashed, and blood immediately poured from a wound on his arm. When he looked, the sheen of white bone could clearly be seen through the blood to the open wound. They spent the next couple of hours of that Christmas morning in A&E. Yes, she was a pussycat, a kitten, until you fucked with her cubs! Then she was a wildcat.

In Coventry, they had split up once. He doesn't remember why, just that it had happened at her bedsit, because despite his urgings from him for her to stop, to get away from him, she followed him all the way home. When they met, she had had the coil fitted, when they split up, she had had it removed. When they got back together not so long after they split, he knew this. He knew it when they intimately made up. The runaway train came down the track and she blew she blew…

(Missing – Everything but The Girl) 12 347 711

As the cold winds blew the following year, the plan that had brought him to Coventry in the first place had fell through and she knew he was going back to Middlesbrough that coming March and though they weren't together by this point, they still spent their free time in each other's company. She was 2 or 3 months pregnant. By March, when he left, she was very much showing. By April he was working as a postman with his best friend. As the weeks progressed, he visited her in Coventry, where she had her own flat and had turned her own bedroom into a nursery ready for the arrival of our child. She came up North once or twice and established what would become a lifelong relationship with his sister. As the due date approached, he notified his employers that he would be taking his two weeks' paternity which could be any day. When the due date came and went, he took his leave and left for Coventry. An overrunning pregnancy was further exacerbated by a complicated birth. Mother didn't dilate enough and the child, seemingly happy within the womb of her mother, would become distressed when she was ready to arrive but couldn't. They were rushed to another room for a C-Section and an hour later she was in his arms and never, ever, had he felt such love and relief. This change, he did feel.

He visited his daughter every week. He was happy to see her too, he missed her, but his duty was to his child and this status quo remained in place for some months. Until one day, he was about to leave, feeling the pain in the back of his throat, the suppressed painful emotion of leaving her again, saltwater rising within him, (His ex would usually leave him to it at this point. He can't remember whether this was at his own request.) and his daughter looked at him and in those sad blue dewy eyes they seemed to say to him, scream at him: "Dad, please don't leave me! Please don't leave me!"

And as tears dropped like great selfish splattering bombs upon his body, after today, he made the decision to never leave her again.

"Leave this with me!" He said mysteriously to his ex as he departed and once home and after several conversations, phone calls and a holiday from work he was stood in the kitchen of her father's home in Coventry. He was giving the talk.

"They are yours to look after now. Make sure you take care of them." She bid farewell to her family, her father and stepmother, younger sister and twin brothers and that night the 3 of us spent the night in my bedroom in my mother's house in Middlesbrough. A few days later they moved into his sister's house. They got engaged, but there was no party, this was a different kind of bond. Within a couple of weeks, he had secured a loan from the bank, and they moved into their first family home. He had made a commitment to himself, to them, and he was determined to see it through.

(Ready or Not [Champion Bootleg] – The Fugees) 23 167 075

The relationship, at least in the early years, was a lesson in parenthood, shared enterprise. They loved each other, that was clear, but they loved their child more. That is generally the case in most relationships admittedly, but it is often left unsaid. A base, like ground, like Earth, like the fundamental function of the spine on the skeleton. In this relationship that particular truth was never hidden. It was the base and the ether, the ground, the Earth, the sky the air, the spine, the brain, the heart. It wasn't just the singular line that held the fabric of the relationship together, it was the fabric of the relationship itself. In retrospect he wonders whether this factor contributed to the downfall of the intimacy that is supposed to be enjoyed by the coming together of a man and a woman. That somehow, we both neglected the emotional, physical and spiritual union of one another as sovereign, as ego, as stand-alone entities within a dynamic of family life. Whether we were right or whether we were wrong, we loved each other until the end and remained lifelong friends. One day, after the death of her mother, my daughter, who is now herself a mother, said to me that she wanted hers and _____'s relationship to be like the one shared by myself and her mother. I guess there is no bigger compliment than that!

Despite neither of us having a religious background or upbringing our daughter was christened in early 98. Despite his antithesis towards the vain pursuit of body sculpting he joined the gym and went regularly. (Okay, for a man who saw lots of grey areas he initially saw this as vain. He came to realise that of course there are more benefits to a healthy lifestyle and body than just the vanity of it!) Despite her antithesis for education, she joined a college course. By mid-1998 we had moved to another rented home, complete with jacuzzi bath and tree house – obviously big selling-points. She took driving lessons and passed first time, they bought a car, he had another crack at education and joined the local University while continuing to work on the post. He cooked because she couldn't cook for shit. She cleaned because he didn't give a shit. On the surface all that was missing was the white picket fence. Scratch below the surface and it is often a different colour, different texture, different material. Cracks were showing and a symbiosis can only last so long once the boredom sets in. Her self-confidence was growing and that was good, for one once so addled with insecurity. Her vanity grew and so did her need for attention and that was a problem that stacked up the house of cards ready to be blown down. Sometimes the basis for the beginning of a relationship possibly has some subconscious bearing on its ultimate demise. He never feels like he made her feel wanting throughout their relationship. He certainly didn't go chasing or consciously blow smoke up the arse of another. Her need for external attention, he is sure, certainly wasn't based on any impropriety on her part or any conscious future infidelity. A ball rolls and it gathers speed and momentum and so it is sometimes with attention wherever it may come when it is not always so forthcoming from the one you love. No single incident broke the relationship, just a constant and ever-increasing flow of paper straws. He left her in 2001. The books he had read on property acquisition whilst they occupied their first address paid dividends when he bought a repossessed flat some months later for thirteen grand.

(Family Portrait – Pink) 91 828 214

It's 2020 and they are talking.

"You said you would sign your flat over to me if we got back together!" The man snorts and shakes his head.

"Are you for real?" He knows he didn't or if the words did leave his mouth, it was without substance or true conviction. "Don't be so fuckin stupid!" She protests, laughing.

"I swear, Darl, you did…" He looks at her and she grins before placing a finger to her mouth and licking the end before tracing a 'one' in mid-air. "One, one." She giggles and he laughs and shakes his head: "You were good… But not that fuckin good!"

While the flat is being finalised, he moves into his best friend's flat. He has already bought his. They devise a plan; this one might just work. Two men with brains and ambition, regular income, living the single men's dream. His friend rents out his own flat to his older brother, his own mortgage paid with some left over, and they move into the new flat. The man has a job, a flat with a pittance of a mortgage to pay and covered by the rent paid to him by his friend and then… She moves in. It is a reconciliation of bodies only, the Coventry gang back together 5 years after it began. This time the two have become three. What could go wrong? Paint a picture, paint a sea, paint the sky, and make sure there is plenty of black and grey in the palette, a splash of yellow and red and make sure you add plenty of green. More rent, more money, he finishes work before noon every day. He takes a second job at the sorting office. Split shifting. Now, when he wakes at four, he doesn't know which job he is supposed to be going to. More money. He could invest it wisely, he could, he is clever, but he lacks patience, fortitude. He's a runaway train and he has re-established a love affair with horses and the racing of them. The internet is growing in sophistication. He has six tabs up, horseracing form, commentary, he is at the racecourse, in the betting shop, in his ears. He has found a home for his surplus cash. Staying up late, painstaking trudging through information. What are you looking for? The Formula. There is NO formula for this! He isn't waking for work. Stop… Stop. He is so busy, busy with… He's getting on with it, with what? She is getting on with life, with love maybe. He is too busy for either, except notice she isn't, like a sour whiff under his nostrils. His best friend buys a house in the centre of Town, he is staying the course. He moves in, he is staying the course too – but only in body. Saturn Return in full swing he moves away, London, knowing his mortgage is being paid. When he talks to people about jobs, he's had he always places his job on the post above the rest. Why? They ask. The freedom, he says. Once you leave the office you are your own boss, the sun is on your face and the wind is in your hair. What time you finish is all down to you and your own ability. You ever wake on a morning and just feel the natural high of the Sun streaming through the window as it rises and warms you as you ride to work and knowing that you will be home and finished before it ever even reaches its highest point in the sky? That is why it was my favourite job. Why'd you leave then? I would have stayed there forever! He watches the Twin Towers fall from behind a bar in Muswell Hill. His best friend buys a flat around the corner from his own with his credit card. He is coming home; the wheels fell off there too! She moves into his best friends flat around the corner. Now he has a mortgage but no job. It is perhaps at this point that he made the statement she so adamantly stated. Seemingly loveless, low and alone a man may say almost anything to rebuild the splinters of a shattered ego. He moved into his sister's house who lived in the Yorkshire village in which he was first engaged almost ten years before. He rented out his flat to a lovely young couple that decided to keep the rent cheques for themselves and obtain false credit in his name... But that is another story. The year is 2002.

She remained in his life for the remainder of her own, always on the periphery, almost completely platonic. She never had another child. She used to say that she never wanted children from different fathers. If there was another reason, she never discussed it at any point with him. She loved and she loved deeply. She married, she divorced, she loved and kept on doing so until her death. When he met her, she had an addictive personality. She never hid from that, very open about it in the beginning. Throughout these years she was never consumed by anything that may be deemed as addictive. Unless of course addiction to one's own children is an addiction at all? Then she was an addict. In the end it was an addiction that killed her, slowly but surely but present all the same. It is sad, so sad, but what is worse is that she was too proud to tell anyone what was putting her here but not proud enough to stop it. The Man misses her. He thinks, he will always miss her.

(Go Your Own Way – Lissie) 5 982 450

Nicholas escorted her down dusty streets and small alleyways in the light of a low-hanging moon, like a large white tulip. They talked and laughed giddily and foolishly about nothing and everything that could ever be recalled, in even the moment, only the memory of the reciprocation of a mutual joy in each other's presence and company. She danced as she walked, and she sang as she talked and as they passed the coloured abodes of wood and brick that made up a large portion of the Dutch landscape she skipped up and down the steps of the houses as her reserved English escort watched on. Watched the spirited young Dutch girl beat with increasing rhythm on the bearskin of his heart. He took her hand as she pirouetted like a ballerina down by the canal, the moon's light reflecting off the black water like a shining mirror, and when she lost balance and fell into him, into his body, into his chest, their eyes locked and seemed to stay in that place for an eternity entirely too short. Somewhere, somewhere in the workshops close by, they could hear the hammering of metal on metal. The sound of the ever-increasing progress of the Dutch Golden Age moved on, forward, like the dance stepping of the couple skirting the canal oblivious to the tinkerers and mongers making cannon.

(Only Girl in the World – Rihanna) 851 868 826

There was a girl, the year is 2002. Have you ever been obsessed? Staring at your phone, willing the comforting melody of the ringtone to sail into the air like some sonorous deliverance from an oblivion you feel yourself occupying. Is it love? Is it love? It's in the ballpark, the outer edges of the key, scrunched in the line of the Venn Diagram. A dark cloak at a colourful fashion parade, the Goths at a sports game. Sometimes, he would hear his ringtone and move excitedly towards the source only to discover it's the song on the radio. Phone flies. Man wanders sulkily: 'Lonely as a cloud that floats on high o'er vales and hills, when all at once he shouts out loud, fuck you, fuck your mother, fuck your brother, fuck your lover, or significant other, fuck you and your cheap thrills.' Not sure that's the words... Resurrection was his ringtone, but this one tried to kill him.

He knew. Knew from the off. She said to him a few months after they met: "Do you know what you said to me the first time we met?" He couldn't remember, they'd met in the pub in the Yorkshire village. He shrugged his shoulders. "You said to leave you alone because I was far too good looking for you!" Yeah, he thinks, I must have been wasted because I'm not that shallow. She was older than him by some way, about 10 years, but she was stunning. Not in the traditional sense. She was stunningly different, attracted men like some giant gyroscopic magnet mopping up small filings. She was different and she was disliked by so many women and the families of men captivated by her catwalk gait, her swishing, lithe frame and bohemian wardrobe, flowing in the judgemental ether of the small hearth-based British Country pub. He liked her, fuck, he must have done he was dodging knives to talk to her. Whatever he said it worked because she invited him back. Nothing happened. She was seeing someone else. Thanks for telling me love, might wanna slip that info in early doors! Who? WHO? Great! I'm about to be a pariah like you. One thing he remembers about that particular night was her extremely large wardrobe and absolutely fascinating array of belts which in his drunken state he felt a compulsion to try on much to her delight. She laughed and it spurred him on, he so wanted to make her laugh. He had entered her life. Must have been Cerberus's night off.

(Resurrection – PPK) 978 786

Within a few days she had him hooked, like Ares in Hephaestus' net. When the boy she was seeing entered her bedroom and saw that I was sat in it, he looked at me like Brutus had just thrust the knife into him. I knew him, had known him for many years. We weren't friends but I think we liked each other, and he was immensely popular in the Village so this little event wouldn't do the man's own popularity any good, especially as he was viewed as an outsider anyway despite his paternal sides deep-rooted association with the place. He didn't say anything, and we weren't in any kind of compromising position, but he looked hurt. Hurt at me, hurt at her and then he left. He was about to say something when the laugh that she had obviously been supressing poured out of her with the cacophonous echo of what was about to come. He didn't know it then; he knows it now. So that was that. The end of that relationship? This was the really clever part of her manipulation. She never actually black and white told you she was with you. If a relationship could be deemed as 'spending time with' that was the flexibility of her dynamic to relationships. She had one rule, her own list of them. Incidentally, some years later, the man in question did go on to be my sister's first husband. Ironic. Karmic. Whatever, I liked him anyway, am not my sister's keeper and I was happy for them and their loving if brief matrimonial bliss. I even attended the wedding and would go on many nights out with them in Middlesbrough, so if he harboured any grudges, it never showed and neither of us ever mentioned this particular night or the girl in question ever.

Her lure? Come on. Every girl with a brain cell knows the weakness of a man. Fuck, even men know that girls know the weakness of a man and yet, still, we choose to jump from the rocks into the temperate pools of that carnal bliss. She could fuck. No, really, she could fuck! They were making love once, having sex, fucking rampantly with her head threw back, eyes closed, mumbling, whispering, incanting, whatever, when she says clear as day: "My Mother always said stay with the one that fucks you like…" Or words to that affect. It may break the man's stride for a stroke or two: "What did she just say?"

If this offends, the choice is simple, stop reading. It is a re-telling, not a generalisation. It may seem discourteous to not offer her a chance of reply. Believe me, if I sent her this, she wouldn't hate me for a second until she'd asked if it had been published and how much she was getting for her inclusion in it! People who steel-cap over the bodies, hearts and souls of men and women alike with mercilessness are extended no courtesy from me. Her very inclusion is a testimony to a lesson learnt, which is a key point of this text, not an acrimonious and bitter stripping of her character. The truth is, she was the worst person I ever loved and ever loved fucking and it is my democratic right and privilege to say that!

The Man's stride is further broken when sometime later he reads a book she has loaned to him entitled:

London Fields by Martin Amis, and the central character, the protagonist, quotes the exact lines she quoted to
me whilst being fucked. Stadiums full of Communist
flags are waving in a torrential storm but he is too busy
looking away, looking away, eyes splayed upon golden
hay.

(Maneater – Hall & Oates) 179 480 173

It's dark but not cold. The only chill he feels is the
one within his soul. He feeds hungrily on the fish and
chips clutched in the fingers that just a couple of hours
before were learning to competently and gracefully slide
chips across a roulette table. As he comes to the bridge,
he sees a rat the size of a cat clamber out of one of the
holes in the wall under it. He wonders how he got
here… Here is Selly Oak, the student area of Birmingham. Large house upon house, upon house, along long
street upon street upon street. A ruthless landlords'
goldmine. A real-life monopoly money-maker. He
hopes they are not in. Any of them. He wants a bath and
could do without the second-degree lecture about the
cost of hot water. At least he is eating. If Birmingham is
good for something, it is at least good for the value of
the food. A full boat of Britain's traditional for less than
two quid! The casino only gives you sandwiches for
dinner and the 8 mile walk to and from only serve to
burn that off your body like a fire-lit crisp. This, this,
this salt and vinegared little mass of yellows and gold is
the only thing good in his day at the moment and he
forces it into him like Prince Tramp. He is close to
home, but the length of the street is interminable. God,
let them be out! Sometimes we would bear the black

looks of disapproval and go out to the pub in the village. Never together, just together, because apparently there was another man in her life. He was older and worshipped her and he wanted to fuck her, but he never did. So, he meets the foil, the fool. So, who is he? I hope she doesn't see me as the fuckin Keith character; I don't even play darts, but I am a savage, or will be in her eyes. At this point I have no money because I'm lurching from temporary job to job. A bit of piecework at the printers. I'm living on my credit card and a diet of Indian takeaways and a bottle of red wine every time I am not with her. I walk into my sister's living room with said items upon a platter: "Look at you," she laughs. "Lord Muck!" Will Young has just slated Simon Cowell's comments on his performance. "Go Will!" Northern English, common, skint, don't confuse that with a lack of intelligence bitch! But I was. For this period. Unintelligent. She tells me in her eloquent Southern accent how she hates her mother, but she has a million-pound flat in London, her dandy father and his young family and property in Cyprus and her professional gambler ex, father of her son, who, for the record was an absolute credit of a human being. Let's not forget that she went to school with Britt Ekland and Peter Sellers' daughter, and you have a whole bag of interest. A well-rounded protagonist for her own story.

"I'd love another," she says, playfully flirting with the foil. "And Lee will have one too!" The foil looks at him; the Man looks back dropping his glass on the bar.

"Much appreciated…" The foil looks at him like a father would look at his son. If he fuckin despised him.

The street is orange, and the atmosphere is golden. Warm roads, cold glasses, smiley happy people all around. Horns honking at the groups sat outside the pubs, at least four of them, all on the high street. The Yorkshire Village is a wonderful, glorious place in the height of Summer. My Mother and her partner of a thousand years are sat outside one of them (Yes, they live here too! Small World this ain't it?) with my sister as he heads on down the high street crosses the road and greets them. His at-some-point-to-be stepdad, because eventually they do get married, buys the round and maybe another before he heads to the cash machine, credit card in hand. Declined. He tries again. Declined. He walks over to his family smiling: "Declined my card," he says. Then philosophically. "The party is over!"

(Light My Fire – Will Young) 737 905

He had options. No, he had an option. He never had any option he was always going to go with her. She had discussed the possibility of moving on and I imagine the panic on the man's face must have been palpable, but she asked him to come with her; so there had never really been an option. He was going. Whatever anyone did or said that would have tried to aid and dissuade this ill-informed decision, he was going. I had nothing but me, I had no money. It was the only time in his life he ever really wanted some and thought of several - some fraudulent – ways to acquire some. If that wasn't a big red flag, like the application of a breath-squeezing polythene bag upon his face, he didn't know what was. He never embarked in any fraudulent behaviour, unless ignoring one's intuition could be deemed as such and moved to Birmingham with her, her teenage son and his teenage best friend, who spent more time in the company of his surrogate parents than his friend himself. One big happy intelligentsia. They docked at Selly Oak. Three bedrooms; 'We are going to need a bigger boat!' One for you two, one for you, one for you. He relied on her to keep him, only time in his life. Sometimes a bottle of red wine would appear.

"I know you like your wine!" She had a way of saying it that suggested he was both a child and an alcoholic all at the same time. Some key in her voice, some glorious intonation, some look of satisfied disapproval. The spikes of the beat up and over and plummeting down and below the flatline. He got an interview for a job as a croupier. She was delighted, the promise of money, her face ignited.

Have you ever overheard a man, sometimes not even overheard, talk to a woman that he wants to be with? Especially those that are good at it. It is at once laughable and grudgingly awe-inspiring. How the bullshit rolls, like a stampede of incontinent cattle, you laugh at the incredulity of it, the shallowness of the lie. And then the mouth falls open when you see, the woman, laughing, flirting back, enamoured. You do a double take and look at the man, up and down from every angle. There must be something. Looks? Delivery? Some unseen pheromones? Because, surely to God, she has not just believed a word he has just said! The art of the lie! Just agree. Agree! You like that too… Yes, you do, I do, but I can't stand it! Agree. Fuckin agree goddammit! He remains silent a lot of this time, because he knows what she really likes, and he can't provide her with it. Not yet, at any rate. Pretty words and agreeable affirmations are not going to do it. Was I wrong? How could I have been so wrong? Education was wasted on me. They never taught you how to talk to a woman, sport, that ain't in the curriculum!

He is drinking in the bedroom they currently share, not their bedroom. He is halfway through croupier training at this point. A position that requires six weeks. SIX WEEKS of unpaid employment before they (might) take you on. It must be his day off. Red wine is taking effect and he is morosely listening to music, headphones in. Bowie, who he loves anyway. But also, Placebo and Bran Van 3000. She got him into them! I agree, I agree! We do have a mutual enjoyment for something that is not based on some lie I have conjured to enamour. But it is too late. No point arriving stage left when they have already exited stage right. He looks around, alone on the stage, spotlight on him and then the audience begin to laugh. Raucous belly-busting laughter. He has realised the truth. Yes, it is not paranoia. This is happening!

(I Know – Placebo) 164 795

The next 24 hours show the Man's mettle. Torpedo in the hull, does he sink? They come in. He hears them. He is laid on the bed, appears to love this position at crisis point. It's not crisis point. That has gone and passed. From the first moment he thought it to this. This is crises point, crescendo. She comes in the room, and they argue. She tries to convince him he is wrong. Creak on the stairs. She leaves the room. He hears the kiss. At the time he thought this was designed to further humiliate him. Stamp on his soul. Now, thinking about it, as an adult, as an objective observer of it, I don't think that was it at all. He perhaps came to protect her should it turn really ugly, sneaking about on the stairs listening, making sure she was okay. The kiss? Her telling him she is alright. Perhaps the initial thought, perhaps this one. Who knows. She returns and laughs at him as if he is crazy when he says he has just heard them. She protests, without protestation. He is done. Switched off. He doesn't believe a single word, muscle in her body, so he gets off the bed. Heading for the door he can't remember whether she tried to stop him, to stop him from going, or beating the boy to death with a pan. He goes downstairs.

"____! A word… Let's go for a drink!"

The Man leaves the house and her son's best friend follows. What does he feel? He doesn't feel hatred or that he has been betrayed. All's fair in love and war they say. Why does he not feel the anger? Because relief comes with the knowledge and this boy is open about it. His confusion and disbelief of the scenario over the previous weeks now confirmed and an affirmation that he is not some absolute obsessive, possessive, crazy arsed person. What he believed to be true was true. Why so calm, so assured? Because the cold incisive workings of the mind have taken over; heart has gone on vacay. The Man can see the future, not really, but obviously, and he already feels sorry for this kid. So, they agree. Is it days, a week, weeks? The Man is in the downstairs bedroom sat at his, computer then, as he sits at his laptop now. Shaking his head. ____ is on the sofa. He did occupy her room, until now. Now she is dating somebody else. That had been the agreement that day. The Man had lost, he knew that. There was no going back from this, so other than scuttle off home, tail between his legs, what was there to do? We move bedrooms tonight, agreed? Of course, he agrees. Boy about to get laid! Does he feel sick about it? Of course, he does. At least they had the courtesy to be quiet. In truth, he never heard them at any point. He is almost through croupier training, and it would be a travesty to throw that away. He has a plan. Now he is a valet (posh word for free drink server) in the casino as he awaits his gaming licence, should he be successful in his application, then he has the job as a croupier. Now he is earning, but not yet paid. For a while there she made him feel useless, inadequate, that he wasn't worthy of being in a relationship, despite the fact he had spent most of his adult life in them. He hears a car pull up outside and then zoom off, all exhaust. She enters the house and then his room with a bottle of wine and glasses. They have a drink as she sits on his mattress, and they talk and laugh, and it is enjoyable. He hasn't had a drink for a while. It's refreshing that she is actually being nice to him because over the past few weeks, pardon the French, but she has been a cunt! Moody, spitting words at him, entering when he's having a bath: "How long are you going to be? I need to get ready!"

"When you getting paid, you owe…" Etcetera, etcetera. Civility has returned and is she… No, she isn't!

"What would you do if I tried it on with you now?" He doesn't think.

"I'd recoil!" She smiles but there is no laughter in her eyes. I think she may even have congratulated me on her way out. You've dealt with snakes love, now try the fuckin mongoose.

The night before he leaves, they are at the pill-club they all frequented sometimes. He is sat in the coffee bar area actually upstairs in the club with ____. They have become relatively close due to, who knows, shared experience. He even walks with him, a mile or two, to work sometimes, talking. As they sip coffee the Man tells him that on the following day he is leaving. He doesn't know why he tells him. Perhaps it is an appreciation that when confronted with the questions he needed answering that time he told him the truth. He didn't believe me, but my bags were in my room, already packed, and I had already secured a house share to move into in Edgbaston. I don't think he told her. I acquired the Gaming Licence and became a croupier in the centre of Birmingham. Some months later I saw her handing out leaflets in the centre of the city. She balled and shouted at me about owing her this and owing her that. Guess I was right: "Fuck off!" I said and carried on walking. I heard some years later they had actually got married; her and her son's best friend. I was a bit gobsmacked at the time but when you agree, you agree, you agree... And he will have had to have done a lot of agreeing however uncomfortable.

(Don't Mug Yourself – The Streets) 22 157 (Dry Your Eyes Mate – The Streets) 5 744 673

They stopped at the end of her row. A more prosperous quarter of the city. "Thank you, Nicholas," she said pulling out a small purse. "How much do I owe you?" He placed his hand upon her purse and lightly pushed it back towards her.

"The pleasure was all mine, Miss Arabella." He looked away. "Next time, next time we'll split the bill…" The words struggled to find their way out of his mouth.

"There'll be a next time?" She laughed and took hold of his chin and pulled his face to look at her. "Nicholas? There will be a next time, ya?" He looked into her eyes, sparkling in the moonlight.

"Of course!" He took her hand from his face and was about to kiss it when she stopped him and put her hand on his chest and quickly kissed him upon the lips: "Goodnight," she said, backing away smiling as she looked into his face, twizzled before hitching her skirt up above her feet and running gracefully towards her house. He stood watching her enter her home and stood still some minutes later in the moonlight before running, tearing his way back to the University, running his cane across the fronts of some houses en route and laughing. Laughing like a child. Laughing like a young man in the throes of love.

(I See the Light – Tangled) 1 922 014

There was a girl, the year is 2003. The Man remained in Birmingham working as a croupier. He loved the buzz of the City, loved the independence of living his own life, sometimes unapologetically. He made some good friends among the Midlanders and the job, as a job itself, was interesting. It was within the walls of the casino that he learnt to perfect the art of the power nap. An hour or two of constant and almost instant arithmetic, a skill he was credited for, (he never was really any good at the chip tricks some of the croups displayed...) can be taxing on the brain. So, every couple of hours you were given a 10-minute break where it was recommended you have a couple of minutes' sleep, especially when doing at least one 16-hour shift before a short return – a shift pattern attributed to him weekly. The wages were diabolical, for what you did, and add in the fact that the UK was one of only 2 Countries where the employees were not allowed to accept tips. Also, I missed my daughter and family, terribly. When they rota'd me in for Boxing Day, meaning I couldn't go home for Christmas at all, and the 3 other housemates were all going home... Well. It is a running joke with my mother every time this subject comes up: "I imagined our Lee, with his frozen Christmas meal for one..." Laughing, she continues: "Blowing his party horn and letting off a party popper...'Merry Christmas everybody!'" It never happened. I rang in sick and came home and had the greatest time, so it was only a matter of time before I returned.

In the Winter of 2003, as Saturn was on the downslope through Gemini - a position it had been at his birth - he came home and began working the Betting Shops again as a manager, shadowed for some weeks by the area manager, who trained me up on the new system that was now in place. I knew her, the area manager, from the previous time and she was good friends with my mother who has now spent the best part of 30 years running Betting Shops. It was while I was with her that the first mention of the girl entered his consciousness.

"You're single, aren't you?" He looked over to her from the passenger seat and may even have frowned.

"Yeah!" "Did you ever meet ____ last time? Lovely girl, works in that shop there..." They passed one of the companies Betting Shops. "She's recently become single too!" Oh, no, no, no, no... This boy is doing just fine thank you. Appreciate the concern and all!

"Really," he replied without conviction.

(Love Song – Amiel) 537 864

Chapter Twenty-four

Liars beware! When facing the countenance of truth, or hypnotised in the eyes of love's gaze, be aware... She is no fool.

There was a girl, the year is 2003 and if first impressions were the foundations on which a relationship was built to last, this one wasn't going to last the season! It was summer in the third week of July, and I imagine it was warm, though I have no recollection, except that every time we ever discussed that first meeting, with each other or in company, Sarah would always comment on the ridiculous woolly polo-neck jumper I wore. (It was a seaside town incidentally!) Not that she was mesmerized by my blue eyes or entranced by my charm and dashing demeanour. It turns out that that is what she was expecting judged on the passing opinion of others.

"I was expecting Brad Pitt!" She would exclaim, as all parties involved would look at me up and down laughing, myself included. "And I got him..." This was a typical example of the brutal and clumsy Sagittarian tongue that the Man would learn to deal with over the tenure of their miraculous seventeen-year relationship; miraculous, because they barely got past the first superficial, judgemental minute. "I love him really," she would continue, planting a sloppy kiss on the side of his face. "Don't I, Babe?" The Man would smile and continue the retelling: "She thought I was gay..."

"I did, I really did," she would chunter in the background.

"I thought she was an up-her-own-arse stuck-up bitch!" He would look over at his wife, shaking his head but smiling all the while as she would usually counter, loud whispering: "I was a bitch, I was, but I wasn't stuck up."

Then as the Man would begin to speak again, their friends listening, their children laughing at their parents. "COME ON… I was expecting Brad Pitt!"

"Not my fault!"

"Brad Pitt…" She'd whisper incredulously, both hands gesturing to the Man like she would present a prize souffle just lifted from the hot oven.

"Not my fault your friends fancied me!" She'd usually giggle at this point and then shake her head in disagreement at this particular section of the story. "Anyway, we pretty much hated each other straight from the off, but couple of hours in, I start to talk to her friend by the dancefloor and so, she, clearly jealous, appeared on the scene and grabbed me on to the dancefloor…"

"No, no, no," she would remonstrate, shaking her head. "You were going to get your head kicked in! I just didn't want…"

"Don't be silly," interjection. "She, (her friend), was one of the ones that told you about me so, clearly jealous, Babe!"

"Honestly, Babe. Her boyfriend was sat looking daggers at you. He was going to kick off…"

"Whatever," the Man continues shrugging his shoulders. "We march on to the dancefloor – Tiffany is on – and we start dancing and there's (Area Manager) already dancing and winking and nodding her head at us both like she is Cilla Black. She always said she was the one that got us together." Depending on the company, would depend on whether or not the Man told them that she left the dancefloor maybe an hour later with a line of love-bites along her chest bone.

"I asked her back to my flat, but she said no."

"Good job," she'd say, shaking her head at the audience. "Shithole… Absolute shithole."

"It wasn't that bad!"

"Shithole!" She'd endorse. "And ___ said you were on the rebound, in the taxi home."

The Man always disputed this because the girl he was apparently on the rebound with, this gem of information on which she was garnished, was the mother of his daughter and oceans of water had gone under that bridge. He never mentioned that he had been in a relationship with her namesake long after that. He never told her that until much, much later. The Man didn't know it yet and neither did the Woman… They had just met their future spouse.

(I Think We're Alone Now – Tiffany) 96 703 455

The Man has a sketchbook resting on his knees; his friend and one of The Lads, who he now lives with in Newcastle has just flicked cigarette ash on the floor. Not exactly Bohemian, more laziness. Is he watching telly or writing up something for college that the Man will type up for him later, on his word processor? His laziness appears to know no bounds, like an epidemic within him. Put him in a social situation and watch that energy fizz, the laziness a dead log within him. He will be Mayor one day, everyone is sure of it, he has a natural tendency to say the right thing to the right people however it may smart with him inside. (He's already Father Christmas for Redcar & Cleveland Council – perhaps Mayor is below him now.)

"Abstract!" He says, as the Man turns his sketch around to show him, a small patch of doodle, a rash of red, black and blue eczema upon the blank sheet. It has taken him days just to cover a small area of the page. Linda Goodman said Pisceans were artistic; she said a great many things with which the Man could relate. He read her book here, the best he had read on the subject of astrological character spring-boarding and assassination. The Man wanted to be a Scorpio back then, he has learnt to love the gentle fish since! But pictorial art may not be his forte, though it does hold a certain fascination to him. If a psychologist could see this picture what the fuck would they think of it? A thousand tiny doodles joined together! Cartoonland? Repressed! Feeling small, but wanting to expand anyway?

"Americans would buy it…" He continues nonchalantly, tapping his pen against his notebook, thinking. The Man's eyebrows raise as he looks at it. "Uhm…" he sounds. Maybe, he thinks as he captures it in the picture. The centrepiece. And his eyes focus in. They do the spin, from height to subject. He used this camera angle some years later when writing a screenplay. It is the opening scene, and the audience sees a large finger only, dispersing clouds and appearing to point at something below and camera spins slowly from the clouds, gathering speed and momentum like a falling sycamore seed, as it focuses on the apparent attention of the finger. A young man and woman lay huddled under a single large oak in the country. Camera equipment is set up on the surrounding countryside; the young man is an amateur photographer, documenter, filmmaker. He is proposing to his fiancée. She says yes and they kiss and camera, moves up slowly and then pans at speed in direction over the lush of the surrounding area. The idea is to suggest the rushing ahead of time and heads towards a location, future location and in like wind, through a window, through the roof and into a spectator camcorder. View is camcorder on happy couple, confetti, walking out of a room and outer view from outside showing adjacent rooms of the civil ceremony. Focuses in on a TV, up high, set in a bar area. Grainy image. Soundless, is of Lily Allen being interviewed. A soundtrack is playing all the while.

It is a little abstract, this image, fire-hearth in the middle of his doodle. It is not exactly in a straight line, but unmistakeable, nevertheless. He has doodled a name. Without any conscious awareness of it: "SA-RAH."

(You Only Live Twice – Coldplay) 270 773

There was an excruciating wait between that first and the second meeting. The following day I was working in one of the pokiest, oldest holes of the entire company fleet with one of its longest serving managers, and though she was sweet, the chit chat was like nails down a chalkboard; not only because I was hungover, but because I awaited the excitable wails of the telephone. It is hard to believe, looking back over it now, that we had ever indulged in the initial gameplay of relationship psychology. The emotional sparring of snare warfare. 'Wait 3 days... Meh, meh, bleh!' He had probably seen it in The Rules or something – he had once told his ex that The Rules didn't apply to him: 'You play too hard to get, you ain't getting got.' And here he was on that following day, that longest of days and the phone call never arrived. He knew she knew where he was working, surely, she would ring for even the flimsiest of excuses. Every time the manager lifted the handset from the cradle his ears attuned to conversation listening for her name. She'll ring, he thought, she'll ring. He didn't know until later that she was on a week's holiday.

A word of advice to any men who read this. Never seek an appraisal, an opinion, from your best friend on what she looked like. Better still, don't get so hammered that you can't entirely remember. 'Chunky...' He said. What? Like a fuckin Yorkie the Man thought. Big chunky, little chunky? He had just described a range of possibilities from a van to an eighteen-wheeler. Maybe it didn't matter after all, she hadn't called, and all the possible littlest insecurities crept in; aftershave, dress-sense (ha ha), dancing ability, she didn't like love-bites? Neither do I, neither do I, not on show at any rate... I don't know why I did that! After that one time I only ever gave her them on the arse. The day turned into days and by the following weekend I had returned to the betting shop I was trained in and back amongst the staff that knew her.

"There's a barbecue next weekend at (her colleague's) house if you want to come?"

"Have I been invited?"

"It'll be okay, just come…"

"I don't go anywhere without being asked!" Maybe a day or two later her colleague rings the shop and invites me herself. Stuff going on behind the scenes here.

"Sarah's coming."

"Did she ask me to go?" We have had many disputations about the following. She will claim no such thing.

"Yeah!"

"Okay, I'll be there. Thank you for the invite." A couple of hours before my arrival I go to a pub in town with my best friend and his brother for a touch of Dutch courage, bottle bag in tow. Nervously pull up outside in a taxi. Nice house in a nice area. Slow steps down paved drive. Doorbell. The wife of the property answers and smiles that smile only women ever smile in such circumstance. It is both secretive and circus crowdlike. Present bottle. Cans in fridge. I know some, but barely and only from work. They all carry the same smile. Sarah is out the back, in the garden, and the Man inhales as he makes his way out; about to be mangled by an eighteen-wheeler. He needn't have worried all along. She is holding court, clearly an extrovert and their eyes meet and though she carries on, with her story, with whatever it is she is doing, she is embarrassed – he can see that. But it is a nice embarrassment, a nervous embarrassment, and her smile is all teeth but absolutely joyous. The Man thinks it is going to be a good night after all. The Man is not shallow, but she is no eighteen-wheeler.

"Buxom, you prick!" He thinks to himself. "Buxom!"

(Pretty Green Eyes – Ultrabeat) 2 169 549

According to statistics I have just read, Psoriasis affects 125 million people globally. It appears to be slightly more prevalent in women than men and more prevalent in white than black. 1-3% of body coverage is considered mild; 3-10% moderate; 10% severe. There is no gage higher than severe. Insecure? Heart breaking? Incidentally, I never knew these facts, but I know more about psoriasis than I do about say, The Kardashians.

We hit it off immediately. We must have, because I have no amusing anecdote to the contrary and a few hours later we are making out in her colleagues living room. Her colleague's son walks in and always says he was traumatised by what he saw. Me and Sarah used to shake our heads about his amusing account of that night. I guess if he had never seen a baby feed before he may have been. We go back to Sarah's flat a short distance away and we spend the night together. The Man always thought we had, but according to Sarah we indulged everything else but. The Man tends to believe her account of things because he knows men and women. He knows, if that had been the last time they had seen each other, he would have counted it as a notch, even though he could never really remember and so many years on she had no reason to lie and would probably remember more, so the facts tend to speak for themselves. What he does know is that after that night, despite having his own flat bought and paid for, he became a semi-permanent resident in hers.

How can you remember almost the exact date, time and place of meeting plus first song danced to and not something as important as 'the first time' with someone? Do you remember the colour of the first skittle you tasted? No!? Why not? Because there are so many treats in that little bag and that was the first few weeks, months, perhaps a year of the relationship. If we were both off work, we would spend all day in bed and not sleeping either. Sleeping was a short break in between. How do you remember one from five or five from twenty-five? I sit and deliberate now, in real time, do you remember the moment you saw? I don't remember a single time; the memory doesn't exist within me of ever first seeing her psoriasis, even though she was afflicted with it from plunging neckline to underneath the toenails. If 10% is severe; then four fifths of the body is! The Sun is like a healing kiss to the afflicted areas, and it was summer, but still. I never saw the curve, the knobble, of my fiancé's knees until she was pregnant with our children almost 3 years later. In this period, the psoriasis cleared almost completely. People tend to think it is a dermatological condition and it is true the treatments required to deal with the external effects are dermatological, but it is a blood condition, hormonal. We went to watch World War Z at the cinema when it came out. There is a scene in which the infected run past, avoid completely, a young boy among the throng of fresh feeding frenzy. If Sarah were to walk along a midge swarmed loch, she could do so in resolute peace and tranquillity, hands gently lapping in the Scottish water, free from the ravages of little bitey fuckers spoiling everybody else's time. I know, I've seen it. She laughs as I lift the collar of my T-shirt to reveal a hundred squashed bodies in there. She has an unseen forcefield, impenetrable to those that would think to infect. Many years in I tell her she is a superhero, evolutionary. I can't tell her now, because now is 20 years ago and I don't know enough about her malady yet to give her these words.

I remember she always took the quilt with her when going to the toilet on a following morning and then I remember her laying in a scolding bath almost to the brim and she is crying. The Man walks in and asks her what is wrong! She can barely get her words out and uses her hands to illustrate her body from head down.

"This!"

"Oh, Baby…" Heads touch and she weeps into her bath. In the winter months it was always worse for her but in the summer months it was still bad too and apart from that time I don't recall her flailing under the curse of its sometimes-incredible visual cruelty. She would get angry, sure, but suffer to it, no way.

"Kids are the best," she would say. "I love them. They just come out and ask me." I watched her walk into many a swimming pool, along a beach, drawing the stares. I never told her how incredibly proud of her I was or that she had more balls than me! Give a Fire Sign a fight, right? Fun fact about the Man you won't believe. He used to watch the Kardashians, probably more out of sufferance, can't remember. When I saw an episode where Kim had a fanny fit about a single spot on her leg and wanted to reach into the TV and choke the diva-whine from her spoilt-arse lips, I had to stop watching. I may have been unfair, I don't know, I never watched again to see how the billionaire superstar dealt with it. I only watched every day as my wife dealt with it.

(Beautiful – Christina Aguilera) 140 014 620

The first few years were a lesson in the dynamics of the baggage we each carry venturing into the throes of a new relationship and the messy emotions that come with it. Sarah wasn't long, maybe 6 months, out of an 11-year relationship with her ex-partner with whom she had an 8-year-old daughter, he was still sending her flowers; I was out of a committed relationship with my daughter's mother, now 5, for 2 years but... And I struggle, but what is this if not an honest account? Without the integrity of the author, it is just words zipping across a screen without meaning. There are no bushes to hide in when giving an honest account. Put some pretty flowers in the way of the genitalia and step out into the spotlight. There was never any rebound, that much is true, but in those 2 years, there was sex. Sometimes a man will say: 'It was just sex' and he will mean it and that is fair enough when there are no other parties that can get hurt. When that other party is a human lie-detector, you are fooling yourself trying to fool her. A few weeks after I spent the night at Sarah's she went to Ibiza with her daughter. I don't need to say anymore; we are at the pretty flowers! Let me just say, there comes a point when a man, the Man, makes a heart over cock decision and without ripping off the flowers the Man and his ex-partner never had sex again.

I know Sarah has difficulty believing that because come Christmas, even though she had suspected at least one indiscretion, the Man went off to Yorkshire to spend with his family. His whole family was still in that little Yorkshire village at this time. His ex-partner drove him there – with his daughter, obviously – and stayed there too! Remember, she was best friends with my sister. Nothing happened between us, that much is true. Could I see the full gravity of what I was putting my new partner through? No, that much is true too! I don't think I could see the problem Sarah had with the situation; my ex was well in with my family and her personability had her adored, like a kitten and Sarah's at times acerbic tone whenever we were anywhere in company would have her perceived as the wildcat. Ironically, it was in those private moments that the Man would see the wildcat in his ex and the kitten in his partner, the parts of their personality nobody else really saw. We were out in a nightclub one night, a club my friend who I lived with in Newcastle was the resident DJ, and Sarah and myself were slow dancing. My ex was there too. We began to kiss and within seconds our heads were banged together. My ex had rushed the floor and took it upon herself to dish out some emotional justice. It took every ounce of persuasion on my part to stop Sarah from swinging her around the dancefloor. The story goes that Sarah had clocked her and smiled as we were about to begin our embrace. I have been in both their company, together, because unbelievably a level of civility was reached between them, and the story has been confirmed. In the end, they could both laugh about it, bury the hatchet, usually at verbal detriment to me. But I never minded because I was just content that they were getting along. Sarah had always known. I knew she knew; she knew I knew she knew, and eventually the Man had to admit to his indiscretion. She had almost ended it at crisis point, when we got to crises, she forgave the Man, and the journey would last for 17 years.

(The Boy Is Mine – Brandy & Monica) 69 172 286

I can't remember whether Sarah's dad said the hardest part of a relationship, or the hardest part of a marriage was the first 5 years. It was the first 5 years of our relationship that were certainly the most challenging but also the most exciting. In the August of that first year Sarah went away. In the October I visited my best friend in Germany with another of my good friends and did the Munich Beer Festival. Christmas, I decided to spend it with family – ex-partner in tow on the pretext that she drove me there.

After the failure of two Tests and the death of my friends in a car accident, a car I would have most certainly been in had I not been working away, I suspect I decided that if Death wanted me it would have to find another way. It has always been a part of conversation that the only box a woman has to tick is the ability to drive. A Mantra in the Manter. It isn't true of course, just banter.

And how the sand crunches under one's feet. No need to look in that bag, listen to the sound, feel the grit in your eyes. The point I had always try to make regarding this issue, the issue of the ex, had always fell on deaf ears, in the early years at least, because in order to make the point authentic you must alleviate all the stresses the other person has regarding the point you are making. In that, I failed, and failed miserably because of my own weakness. In principle, it is sound but as I have found talking to many people since, not a populist view. I have spoken to many a man that is not allowed to see their children because of the apparent severity of the separation. (I had children with women who always made it clear that no matter how acrimonious circumstances may stand between us, they would never seek to terminate the father-child relationship. In that, I have been truly blessed with diamonds.) It had always troubled me however that you could make the transition from love to hate simply because you were no longer compatible. My ex was still very much a good friend, despite the breakup, and the mother of my child, so it was in everyone's best interests to retain a level of decorum, in my eyes at any rate. 'You always defend her!' It was true, I did. Sarah believed I had her back over her own and that simply wasn't true, but in order to admit that was to infer that there were people that I had to have her back for! I always used the fact that I was there with her, over my ex, as proof enough that that wasn't true without ever telling her that any detrimental word in her direction, in my company, was met with condemnation. My ex felt many the sting of verbal reciprocation when daring to cross that line. A friend that had the temerity to insult her was cut off and removed from my life completely. That was 18 years ago, and I haven't spoken to him since. I don't know whether Sarah ever noticed.

(You Don't Own Me – Saygrace feat. G-Eazy) 382 519 666

We rode out the early storms and as weeks turned into months and we settled into couplehood my daughter began to spend Saturdays with her dad at Sarah's flat because I had moved out of my own. I used to have her on a Thursday at my flat when I still officially lived there. Now I didn't and had rented it out again and pretty soon the flat Sarah and I were occupying was being sold under her feet, so in the March of the following year we moved into our first accommodation together as a couple.

Those first couple of years; the getting-to-know-you stage of any relationship is going to be the signal-point, the knowledge-bank and intuitive feelers of the life and length of it. It isn't rocket science, is it? If you fundamentally disagree on most things, sometimes on just one, but maybe a big one, the discussion is soon going to become less compromise and more conflict. We had our big one and that would always be conflicting, but we also had all the compromises, shared interests and shared beliefs, the attraction and of course the falling in love, which inevitably becomes deeper the further in you go. We had a lot to work with and when we ignored the elephant in the room, stayed out of the jungle, the routine of daily life was great. We worked at the same company, doing the same job, though in different offices. She was established in her own office; I applied for a couple and eventually secured my own; money was decent, and we worked hard, but we played hard too. It is probably fair to say those early years were entirely too drunken but probably established one of the most contributing factors to the life of the relationship and indirectly led to the biggest decision of it.

In August, we had a holiday to Turkey booked and the night before we flew is a prime example of the perils of just too much. We went out for the day, a full session at the local pub just along the road from where we were living. It was a good day, drinking, playing pool – I think I promised her a monetary sum for each ball potted, I was quite good, and this is one of the contributing factors, we liked each other. We genuinely liked to be in each other's company, socially. We enjoyed being out together. We enjoyed being in together too as a couple, but when we were out, we were each other's best friend and that was a factor that endured for the entire relationship. Even when we knew our marriage had failed, the social aspect of the relationship remained. Still, to this day, whenever we attend one of our son's gigs, we do so sitting or standing together with myself still expected to attend the bar. It is not written in stone, but it is what we do. This day, obviously already packed for the upcoming holiday, we spent the entirety of it in the pub and then staggering the short distance home to which we discovered we had lost the house key! Fuck, fuck, fuck! What to do, what to do? Day before holiday, probably eleven to midnight, no access to the property. Light-bulb moment! If the lightbulb is a cracked, black, sulphurous diagram of such. Bedroom window is open, I'll climb in. Sarah interlaced her fingers and, foot in, I climbed onto the overhead canopy of the front door and pushed the horizontal part of the bedroom window to full capacity soon realising that the gap provided wasn't even spacious enough to get my head through. Fail. Get down. Getting up was easy, getting down not so because the canopy is quite high and there is going to be that moment, should I choose to step down the way I had come up, one foot in interlaced fingers, where, extremely intoxicated, I am going to be suspended in mid-air. Make sure ambulance is on speed-dial. Fuck that! "I'm going to hang; you are going to have to catch me, okay?" We've all seen the trust programmes. Lay back, we'll catch you. Rarely is there a 2-foot jaggedy wall in the equation. The Man sees the wall, looming several feet below him and his drunken partner a couple of feet further up. "You NEED to catch me…" 'Okay.' The Man hangs and drops, and the pain is how he would imagine the early stages of being burnt at the stake. It is the stubbing of the toe, the movement to disorient the pain – nobody stands still on toe-stubbing – without the humour and the small wrought iron front gate has been launched off its hinges. The momentum of launching it forward has caused it to come back and land on Sarah's foot. She is in physical empathy, and they argue, out there, day before a romantic holiday for two, in the street. A man from over the road, unhappy with the noise, is told to mind his own business but kickstarts the couple into repairing the damage. Gate is re-installed onto its hinges. I'm assuming Sarah did what we should have done in the first place and rang her dad to bring the spare key over. I'm assuming because I can't really remember the solution, just the problems. The Man and the Woman went to Turkey the following day. The Woman with a swollen foot, the Man with wall-scraping werewolf scratches and a yellow bruise the entire length of his shinbone. It didn't affect their ability to dance; on bended knee with a rose in clenched teeth, acquired moments earlier, in a nightclub in Turkey, the Man proposed, and she said yes. The ring was acquired in Turkey – better gold apparently. The joy was short lived when on returning home the couple had 4 weeks to depart the property because it was being sold. Neither believed this considering there had been no viewings and rather that the concerned neighbour had had more than a passing affinity with the owners. There was an engagement party in which I can only remember being told to: "Kindly remove your hands from my daughter's arse!" I apologetically assented to the command and would have done with any daughter's father, but Sarah's had also been an ex-fire chief and not the kind of man you said no to. It was another 4 years before fourth finger left hand got a sister. We moved the following month. Heaven would have to wait for the time being - in fairness it wasn't as bad as we both thought – but we would have to settle in hell first.

(Heaven [Candlelight Mix] – DJ Sammy) 706 692

Hell was a 3-bedroomed terraced in the bowels of the town and described as such because if the area had been likened to a body, then the tightknit row upon row of terraced street leading up to the main hub was certainly the bowel and where we were within the anatomy of said metaphor, was the colon. The lofty titles of the streets lacked the credence of the name because of the reputation that preceded them. Drug dealing, prostitution, burglary, all the low-level criminality, packaged and spotlighted within the tributaries of brick that was this area of town. I can't remember a single incident, bar one, in which Sarah's car had been broken into as I sat feet away from the street playing online poker – my latest whim, as she liked to call them. Fuckers stole the car radio, and they were quieter than my fiancé and I on a night out! So, we probably had to talk that morning as she dropped me at work and then sped off to her own. The conversation had probably centred around us getting out of this place as soon as possible and the decoration and restoration of my flat ready for re-sale. Maybe even that I had won a few bobs at the poker tables. I can't remember why money was so tight at that time that I was entering freeroll tournaments, as opposed to just playing, considering our managerial wages were okay. Logic tells me it is because I was new to online poker, not the game itself, and wanted to learn about it first before diving in and I soon built up a bankroll. But the biggest likelihood is that we needed the money for materials to redecorate my flat and to save up for the deposit and 3-month's rent that we would need should the dream home come up. It was all about location, location, location. Sarah wanted to be close to where she had spent most of her life and I just wanted to be where she was, so wasn't particularly bothered as long as we were out of this shithole area.

It was a quiet time, but we weren't entirely reclusive. One night, quite early in the tenancy we visited the local social club, almost literally across the road from ourselves, for the first time. Bingo and band. Staple of the Northeast club scene. There are certain things a Northeast kid should learn at school, early school, along with their other activities and curriculum. Such as: owning a soda stream does not make that kid better than you. (It was a soda stream when I was a kid, I suspect there have been various derivatives across the ages since then!); that white chalk you see on the street, use, play with, is not actually chalk, but dog shit. Stay away and keep your fingers out of your mush; the PORK parmo is the 'original' parmo, not chicken; but most importantly, you listening kids? This one gonna save your life someday. Never, ever, ever, ever, ever, under any circumstances – bar an absolute emergency – you listening, Brad? Courtney? You never talk, laugh, make a noise above any noticeable decibel 'While the Bingo Is On!' We weren't close but we could hear and see them, the twentysomethings that had never learnt this one rule. The chorus of shushing was deafening and louder than they had been but rather than shush, get up and leave, the noise had clearly been like clapping to them. They were the stars of their own show, and one lady took it upon herself to scold the irritable and insolent children that dared to venture into this particular jungle! The boys laughed off the ranting bingo-gran and continued, downing shots, loving the negative attention, the fact that the show had stopped. Enter sixty-something committee man who would kindly ask the gentleman to leave. They got maybe three or four mocking words out before the committee man pummelled them where they sat; big lobbing blows, one boy with the left, the other boy with the right, until all the other committee men pulled off the original one as the boys slid down their chairs. Turns out the committee man had been bingo-gran's husband. Not one to advocate violence, in fact surprisingly, I detest it, but my fiancé and I shared a look of gawped surprise to which the Man exclaimed: "We might like it here, Sarah!" We didn't, but it wasn't hell, just a shithole and before the tenancy was up, we were out of there. Sarah got what she wanted, and we moved back into her area, onwards and upwards to concentrate on the other shithole. Flat needed patching.

(Mad World – Gary Jules) 167 535 724

On the day we went to Turkey I rang the guy renting out my flat, a recommendation from my ex-partner; he gave me a mouth full of abuse. Ill advised, she fuckin hates me. I kid, she was just too naïve for some people, those with a sob story. I had already been down this road and spotted the signs a mile away. When I moved away to Birmingham, I rented my flat out to a lovely young couple. I made them tea. As in the drink, after the viewing, and they told me about themselves, and I illustrated the various terms. The woman scolded her partner for not putting his cup down on the coaster. She was obviously the brains because immediately I trusted them, her at least, and accepted their excuses – for a time – about non-arrival of the rent cheques. The telephone call from Cleveland CID, whilst I was in Birmingham, referencing a number of items I had bought and signed for? in person, including various white goods and a large plasma TV in Middlesbrough, soon told me they were a little less than to be trusted.

"They are obtaining false credit in your name!"

I arrived back in Middlesbrough and watched the next rent cheque drop through the letterbox. There was nobody in the property and they hadn't bothered to change the locks. A few minutes after I had torn open the envelope and stood by the kitchen window a car passed slowly, man's head at the passenger window scoping out the situation, and then at speed when they saw me watching them. I never had to pay anything back and I never saw this delightful couple again or any more of their rent cheques. All I really lost was a couple of month's rent but learnt an invaluable lesson about judgement. This guy, in there now wasn't going to spoil my holiday and as soon as I made the decision: "Fucker is gone when I get back! And no more." My whole being relaxed into holiday mode. On returning, myself and Sarah's dad looked for the tenant; the flat, his parent's house, nowhere to be seen. So, we broke in to my flat – he had changed the locks – and replaced them with locks of our own. Apparently, the guy recommended by my ex had also stolen something from her too. You can't sprinkle glitter on shit and call it a hairband! Never saw him again either.

We moved into a house recently acquired by Sarah's best friend and her husband to be. He had a good job, and it was a safe second home investment for himself considering the tenants were friends. It wasn't in the best condition but imagine walking from postcard of cold, shit ridden beach in England onto one of those golden sand private cove Maldivian postcards and you get the picture. Decorating the flat began in earnest and it is wondrous what cheap carpets and a full internal of fresh paint can do to a place. Sometime, that year, 2005, I sold the flat for 43k, clearing almost 30 grand. We put

25 of it away for our first real home together and in the September of that year went to Florida with Sarah's parents to visit her older brother who had been there since he was 19. He had begun at a software company in the Northeast at a tender age, without qualifications, and was now project managing game development at one of the top software companies in America. I don't remember which one, but I do recall he was working on one of the Batman games. He is still in the USA.

Also, that year, I don't remember whether it was before or after America but certainly after we had discussed the possibility, probability even, that we were going to have a child, I went to a tarot card reader. It wasn't planned, but a customer to the betting office had mentioned that he had booked this guy for a party of 10 and one of those had dropped out. I was open-minded so I volunteered to fill the spot. In a town where tarot card people were probably seen as cat owners with cluttered rooms dotted with gnarly half-burnt candles, I think he was surprised, but I think it was myself that would turn out the most surprised. For one, it was a man; a gay man as camp as Christmas who reminded me of one of the Inspectors at the casino who myself and another guy would go out with sometimes after work. Certainly, the funniest person I met in Birmingham. The first time we went out with him, and he took us to a gay bar in town, he must have been at the bar or the toilet or something, a bald beefcake in a tight-fitted white T-shirt came over to our table. We must have stood out like oranges on a plate of apples. I always joked that I was never stylish enough to be gay, but we were in our casino uniforms this night. He leaned, both hands on the table: "Why do you straight men keep infiltrating our bars?"

Infiltrating! Yup, that was the word he used. Protective, muscular guy with brains, balls and a vocab. Damn my aesthetic! "We are with Sean, (I think) he…" And he appears and they chitchat like old lost school buddies that hadn't seen each other in like forever. It was always a good night on the town with Sean. So immediately I liked this guy and barely into it he knew the astrological signs of both myself and Sarah, said we were going to be married and then frowned and said: "You are going to have child(ren), probably twins. Yeah, twins." He didn't influence the idea; it had already been there and in the November, she stopped taking her pill. "It takes 3 months to get out…" On New Year's Day the twins were conceived. You don't need to know how I know just know that I know what I know. When discussing the price of the house we were in, had been paying rent on for over a year, we felt it was over-priced for the quality of it. No mates rates. House hunting began in earnest.

(Rent – Pet Shop Boys) 8 093 185

The year 2006 was the most heart-wrenching and joyful years of our relationship and one moment within it will forever be the most difficult a human being can ever experience. I'm sure I speak for Sarah too. Before the first scan I would touch her stomach and joke about the possibility of there being twins in there. "Little Ronnie and Reggie." I'm no gangsta, but those were the only famous twins I knew that she knew. Had I had said, Apollo and Artemis or Remus and Romulus, I would have been met with a blank stare of contempt followed by: "Dick!" or "I don't want to know…" Truth is she probably already knew but rather refused to indulge the often leftfield thinking of her fiancé. Despite a belief in ghosts and other supernatural oddities she is largely a practical woman and the only time any mythological terminology ever popped up usually concerned the mystery of how my boxers and socks managed to find their way into the washing machine from the bedroom floor.

"Fairies do it? No, I did!" How we turn into our parents.

The midwife covered her belly in a cold jelly and the machine scanned away as we looked on, not really knowing what we were looking at. "Ah," she says and goes over again. "Do you have twins in the family?" No, we said in unison. "You do now!" I think Sarah cried. Two! High five to tarot guy, he nailed it. We are going to need a bigger car. We got one. A 7-seater. But first, few months in, another scan. Hospital visits few times a week. A heartbeat is lost. And our hearts die in that moment with it. We are sat in the office with the doctor, and she says something that is like having a nail gun pressed into your ear and firing so that every part of your brain becomes numb, while your heart is being pulled out by a rough raking instrument.

"There is the possibility you may have to sacrifice one, to save the other."

She didn't just say that! Not happening. We didn't say much to each other that day but as parents she summed up the emotion for both of us: "I can't do it, Babe. I can't do it!" And there were tears and there was heartbreak. The following day we returned and resolved to let nature take its course. You don't know relief, or anything close to it, in the same country as it, until you hear them say: "It's okay, the heartbeat is back."

It had been something to do with the umbilical cord that our daughter had managed to get a hold of; a grip on, that prevented the machine from reading her properly. They got to the 32 weeks required, maybe a little more, and the Man is sat holding his fiancée's hand as they carve upon her stomach and their son quietly arrives closely followed by their daughter who seemed to bungee out. They weighed three and a half pound each exactly and needed to be fed up the nostril for a while. After a few weeks they left the hospital and a few weeks after that they arrived at the home, they would spend their first 10 years in.

(Speed of Sound – Coldplay) 218 799 341

It was Miller Time and the Man got up and unceremoniously announced he was going for a pee. Miller Time was the time Sarah and I had allotted as the earliest time we could have an alcoholic drink when on holiday with her parents and it stuck with successive holidays with the kids. 4pm was the time in Majorca on this occasion and we sat at a table outside as a cold wind blew around the complex; it was unusually chilly. An hour before, the lifeguard had cleared the pool of people. Those that questioned were given the demonstration of a single finger moving in circular motion. We couldn't hear what he was saying but saw the gesture and thought nothing of it. The twins were asleep in the buggy with their grandparents just inside. Clearly tired from toddling all day; they learnt to walk properly here. Sarah's daughter was sat at one of a row of computers in an area attached to the main bar. There was a toilet stall attached to the main building, a few seconds from where we were sitting.

"Won't be a minute!"

Had I been much longer than a minute... I was in the middle of business when the main entrance door slammed open, and I half expected to turn around and see someone fall in. Nobody. It closed, slammed open again and I moved. Quickly I headed for where Sarah was supposed to be sitting but she was gone, and the resort was deserted. The main doors to the bar slid open and two shirted men in black trousers ushered and pulled me in urgently before slamming the door and moving away from the entrance. What followed was a torrent of nature. Sheet rain made vision almost impossible except for the lightening which flashed constantly like the flicking on and off of a light switch and white plastic sunbeds sliding and being hurled at the doors and the windows, and they weren't light. It was both scary and fascinating to watch and could have lasted for hours but it didn't, because what we had just witnessed was a twister tearing through the complex. Passing through with conscious-less power. The twins slept through it all. When we surveyed the damage a little later, every sunbed that had been touched by it ended up, in a single line, like a leisure bed totem pole in the centre of the pool. There was even one of the lighted posts in there, the other, some distance from where it had once been, ripped out of the concrete. It was clear, had I been much longer and caught out in that I would have ended up in

Oz. There's no place like home. There's no place like home...

Home was now a 3-bedroomed semi up the road from where we had just departed. I used to say that I let Sarah have all the little decisions in life; the remote, shopping, decorating etc. etc. 'But when it came to the BIG decisions!' He states in a loud, gruff, manly voice. It wasn't true, because 2 months after the twins were born, we moved into a house that I had never yet seen! 25k down on a 120 grand house. This wasn't London, you got more than a shed space up here in a decent area. Sarah had viewed the property, probably while I was at work – knowing she had a viewing, of course – and had taken her dad who is polypractical. I can turn my hand, I think, to a lot of things when I put myself into it. DIY was never one of them. How many Pisceans does it take to change a lightbulb? None! One is in the hospital after getting electrocuted and the other just burnt his fingers on the bulb and dropped it, whereupon the female tutted, picked it up and put it in herself. My stepdad is also a Piscean and we once embarked on putting up a shed. I think it was dark when we finished and there were two boards of wood left over which we both looked at with puzzlement before hiding them under the shed we had just built so that mam didn't see. Plumbed an electric oven in without turning off the mains, my arm was an electric eel. Exploded radiator pipes from the boiler with the pressure gage; if I turn this nozzle, pop, hssss. Flat pack furniture I would lay out, make sure all the pieces were there and crack on. I couldn't do instructions on these things because they gave me lockjaw of the brain. Sat slavering on the mahogany veneer beneath me. You ever assembled bunkbeds - hours with pipes and screws - only to realise that on the last piece you had put it up back to front? Hand up, I'm that guy, twice! The picture is clear; my input would have been as useful as my ability in this arena. Sarah knew what she wanted, her dad is a DIY zen master, I trusted their judgement. A bottle of champagne stood on the mantel-piece with a note attached; 2 words.

"Good luck."

There were a few words missing.

(Our House – Madness) 25 429 833

We shared the responsibilities of our children. If sharing is 75-25. I'm being too hard on myself 63-37. I could change nappies; I'd done that 100's of times be-fore. Never with an object in the middle though, but I was a man so not really a problem. Could never really do sick, snot or bogeys. Okay, sick at a push. Streaky epaulets on each shoulder of my work shirt, baby-wiped to look like shoulder sweat. Sergeant Major Dad! Still don't do snot and have a phobia (not medically) of tis-sues, especially snotty ones. When one of them woke for the night feed I had been assigned – Sarah went up early, I stayed up late, so got the last before dawn – the other was gently awakened. If I'm doing it once, I'm doing it in stereo. So soon learnt the art of children bal-ancing and bottle feeding simultaneously. We both worked full-time jobs, so it was difficult having babies again, but not insurmountable and as we did our own ro-tas, we tried to offer Sarah's parents as much reprieve as possible. By the time the children could walk, despite always saying we never needed to, I think we may have discussed the idea of getting married. The delay between the children and the actual date may have been a financial one but that was taken out of the equation when Sarah's dad offered to finance the civil ceremony we eventually attended. We merely had to pay for the rest. Plenty of time to prepare; a wedding item on the checklist would be ticked off each pay day. By the time the children could talk and in June 2009 we became husband and wife.

By now we had been together for 6 years, engaged for 4. Nothing really changes. Except the beauty of the day captures a memory in which almost everyone got along. We still argue on our wedding night, as we always did in drink, so nothing changed there. I blame Google for most of the arguments we ever had. Once upon a time when a man and woman argued, whilst out in drink, to find the answer to the discussion - Who was the first? Blah, blah. It was…! No, no it was…! You have no idea. I'll prove it tomorrow when I look in the Encyclopaedia Britannica. Of course, that never happened because then you were both sober and didn't give a shit. I hated being wrong and Sarah hated me being right. Google. How she hated that self-satisfied grin across my face and how she laughed when the banana turned upside down. Google, ban it for nights out.

Nothing changes, does it? Yes, it does, and it is something I don't know whether any other man has noticed because I've never heard it expressed before. It is the ring! My, Precious. I don't think a man expects anything too deeply from the wedding, especially when the couple have been in union for so long. Then, the Man is presented with a ring and following this, I don't know whether it is true with any other man, he finds himself using his left hand more. Perhaps, he is just noticing that he is, but he is pushing that shiny, golden band into the face of people like he is presenting warm bread. The change is the external. A woman has already felt this, she has the engagement ring. The man, his bare fingers indicative of nothing to the stranger, the impartial observer. Now, he has a status, a symbol, of belonging – not as in property – but of emotional value to somebody else. Don't psychoanalyse, I have never been neglected and I have always been blessed by love by the people and kin around me, but this is different. A soft leaf, fluttering and laying gently, in the warm dewy grass of your heart with all the rest. 'I promise to…I promise to…'

"Ah, you're married?"

"Yeah, just." (What you don't say: "And we love and see the value in each other on all levels.")

The pinnacle of the whole relationship; Man with flag in hand, reaches the summit and takes a deep satisfied breath as he thrusts the pole into the apex of that mountain, was exactly a year from our wedding. Our first anniversary, as she gave out a little squeal and moved off the chair and into my arms has myself a little choked even now. 7 years in, which is humorous because dad always said that the body changes, goes in 7-year cycles. He never told his children this, we heard it from his long-term partner. She has just finished watching the video I made for her, she is already wearing the Eternity ring – 4th finger trifecta – and has reached the

'Paper' part at the end. First anniversary, paper, I got Bryan Adams tickets to an acoustic session at the Sage in Gateshead. A cosy, 2000-capacity arena. I think, for once I showed her that I listened, no, I always listened. It used to annoy her no end how she could talk as I looked distracted and then recite what she had just said. It was the mindfulness. She realised I could listen and be mindful of what I was listening to. Most times, possibly not, but this occasion, fuck yeah! We went in the October and despite the cosy, laid-back, reserved setting and ambience of the venue, she rocked it. She stood and danced and sang, she gave out the biggest whoops. I remained seated smiling up at her and another me watched me watching her and we exchanged looks like 2 children watching a parent enter a dancefloor and be quite good at it. 'Yeah, man.' They nod to each other. Fuck it, let it go, Babe! Where do you go after the pinnacle? You amble, for as long as possible at the top of that mountain waiting for the wings to appear, maybe. Or maybe you only see the pinnacle when the relationship has ended.

(Heaven [Acoustic] – Bryan Adams) 50 412 487

Chapter Twenty-five

So, what is Subliminism? To attribute a label would be to undermine its very purpose, the purpose of the artist.

Any work of creation, creating, be it writing, painting or musical production is almost always going to have a purpose, some underlying intention within the artist themselves which inevitably becomes subjective to the reader, the observer, the listener, anyway. We've all watched a film adapted from a book we have read, maybe produced to some extent, at least collaboratively, by the writer themselves, and felt the rift of difference from their vision presented to us and the vision we held in our own minds whilst reading it. I guess the best that can be hoped for is that people will take something positive from it, something good and ultimately that it entertained. I'm sure Nietzsche is spinning in his grave at the way his own works were used and manipulated to foster a movement and ideology he openly detested. Maybe Weishaupt, too! I don't know, I never knew the man. How he was as a father, as a son, as a brother and a lover. How he was as a worker, as a friend, as a paying patron and as a man of leisure. I only know, as most do, that his organisation has/had mostly been condemned and so, therefore, the man himself – rightly or wrongly is a matter of one's own personal interpretation. It is not my place to judge another man's intentions only to be clear on my own.

So, what is Subliminism, to me? It is an expose, a love letter, a short history of being. Is it a walk through the valleys of one's own consciousness? A pawing into the crevices of his own body? Trampolining through the twists and turns of the gut, sailing the narrowboat across the rivers of his heart; some waters crashing with waves, others with the stillness of a tranquil pool or freshwater river, soaring over the rolling hills and forests of his mind; some lush green and flourishing, others dark and gnarly. The Man hopes that even the darker areas of fact within these pages are testimony to one thing... He is here, living, breathing, free. Free to think for himself, many miles away from the dark places he sometimes found himself in. Free to choose his own path, even if the path leads to a crossroads, a Universal yellow brick road. In that most famous of yellow brick roads the protagonist is confronted with the decision of which way to go. The appearance of the brainless Scarecrow, brainless but clearly with heart and good intention, a metaphor perhaps for the positions we sometimes find ourselves in. Follow the heart is clearly the message the Subliminist Man sees. This led to the protagonist helping the Tin Man, who himself, wanted a heart, which in itself is steeped in irony. To want a heart to use is to have a heart in the first place! He just didn't know it yet. Finally, she helped the cowardly Lion that found the strength to leave the safety and comfort of his own jungle and face his fears in a quest for the aid of another. There are many things I could say Subliminism is to me with retrospective reflection. Yes, it is meant with the best of intentions but in the words of Professor Keating in Dead Poets Society: "Language was developed for one endeavour... To woo women." When talking to a colleague today about almost finishing it, he asked: "Why did you start writing it?" He doesn't think, the surface answer was immediate.

"To impress a girl!" The colleague looks at him but doesn't ask the question sliding off his mind. "Did it work?" Fuck knows mate, he doesn't answer, fuck knows...

(Bohemian Rhapsody – Queen) 1 465 600 246

From that first kiss, a lover's kiss, they were almost inseparable. Every moment of free time was spent in each other's company. Nicholas was a diligent student, always respected the importance the demands of academia placed upon him, but if the truth be known, he never really wanted to become a doctor. It was a path thrust upon him and a label that would dignify his upbringing but not a thing that ignited his passion, made his soul dance. It was a duty and as a loving and devoted son he did it to appease his father. He knew why. He was an intelligent boy and knew the workings of man. He would look at his father sometimes and see the weariness behind his eyes. The faith that was ever present sometimes drain from him, the confidence and charisma so characteristic of the man seep from his body. He would see the same man, place his hand on his book in silent prayer and leave their house re-invigorated and ready to face those that served to crush his spirit. He never spoke of it directly, but Nicholas knew, and he knew why he was sent here, for the highest quality of education, the loftiest of titles: "Sometimes, Nicholas, a man will only see where you have come from, where you have been and not where you are and what you are trying to achieve..." This enigmatic statement, once a mystery to the boy, was clear to the man. His father had been a leather worker and a preacher, a man of respected but humble origin before the spotlight was shone up-on him and the cold, judgemental mechanisms of gov-ernment and politics and self-serving cronyism born within the well-born, a daisy-chain of privilege he was not a part of, eradicated him. Stepped on him. This was democracy, but thousands of years away from that first democracy in ancient Greece, where the opinion of the common man was as respected as that of the educated. Where the common good was held aloft above the greed and self-interest of a minority. Nicholas could see it; his father was buying him a respect he himself had never been afforded.

But swishing and swimming in the lakes and the streams around Utrecht, his love by his side, he didn't care about any of that. How men saw him was because of the way that he was and not because of some label that a proper education would buy him. How she saw him would be determined by the love and tenderness that he would display to her. The prickling thorn bushes of political England were a million miles away from him as he lay in the soft grass of her love, the daisy-chains of her arms wrapped around him as they laughed gaily in the river. Jan was on the bank, sketching and looked up from his work to his friend splashing in the river.

"You feel the fish on your skin my friend!" He laughed and carried on with his sketch. Jan had not left, had no intention of leaving just yet. They had had the conversation on the intended day of his departure. "It appears Lady Sara has become something of a Deus et machina. I think I will be staying ka-put my friend! I was wrong, maybe, maybe not all swans fly away after all." Lady Sara was by his side, drying in the sun from her own venture into the river and eating an apple. She waved at Nicholas and Arabella playing in the river and then dropped her head on the shoulder of her new beau, they were in love too. "I'll race you to the other side!"

"I want a start," she said hopping in the water on one leg in front of him making sure he stood still. "Not yet," she said laughing, and then faced forward quickly, submerged and began thrashing towards the other side.

"Coming!" He shouted, before beginning the pursuit. She was a strong swimmer, but so too was he and they reached the other side of the bank together. He climbed out, crouched on his feet and put out his hands to pull her out. He stood and held her above him and lowered her slowly, as they gazed into each other's eyes.

"Do you love me?" She said.

"Arabella, I would raze Cities for you…" And when they were head to head, they kissed, and he lowered her to the ground. "And I would build them back up in your honour!"

(Part of Your World – The Little Mermaid) 9 462 330

This morning ritual had become a routine he had grown to love. Morning coffee on the terrace of his sea-front property watching the Sun yawn and stretch up over the sea. Jessica sat at the table next to him admiring the view with a wonder and an awe only a child can muster. Until the Sun had pulled itself free of the deep blue ocean would either speak. This moment, sitting here, watching this and watching his little niece watch this, was his favourite time of the whole day. Her telling him what her itinerary was for the day and him doing the same.

"Ugh, sounds boooo-ring!" He would laugh, laugh at her auto-tune.

"Yes, sweet child, it is…" On this particular morning, before the Sun had yet to furnish their eyes with its full glory, she broke the silence.

"Uncle A?" He didn't look at her.

"Uh-huh?" She looked at his profile.

"God must really, really, love you…" He reached, with a trembling hand towards a pair of sunglasses stationed on the table in front of him. Quickly he placed them on as she looked at him. "He must really love you Uncle A!" He looked away, focused on some point in the far ocean and they rolled, and they rolled like a constant volley of cannon fire on the walls of an impenetrable fortress.

"Yes, I think maybe he does…" He said with a cracked voice and an aching in the back of his throat. Jessica took another sip of her orange juice and dropped off her chair and onto the knee of her great uncle. She pulled up his sunglasses and looked at the sad man that would not look at her.

"Don't worry, Uncle A, don't worry," she said with all the reassurance of a mother coddling her hurt and injured child. And the fortress walls fell, dropped, plummeted into the moat with a loud almighty splash.

(Fix You – Coldplay) 514 424 074

Do they know? Do they know? Sometimes, it takes some deep diving. Do the children know how much, how so much, their father loves them!

(Somebody Better – Mascara's Lies) 103

The tour guide stopped at The Monument and placed his hand on the imposing stone structure as the crowd of tourists, mostly American and Japanese, were already taking photographs and moving their phones up and down it.

"This, my friends, is the Monument to the Great Fire of London, 1666, more commonly referred to among the inhabitants of the city as… simply The Monument." As he was about to continue a hooded man approached and stopped amidst his little crowd and listened. He couldn't see the man's eyes for the hood fell over them, but he seemed to be staring intently at him. "Excuse, excu-" The young guide shook his head and continued. "Over here, just yards from where I stand is where the fire is initially supposed to have taken hold…" The tour guide repeated the details of the fire any interested party could have cherry picked from any site on the internet, but his crowd seemed suitably impressed. "Many and much of the London landscape you see today is indebted to this great tragedy including St Paul's Cathedral with its

iconic dome." There were oohs and aahs and nods of assent. "So, there you have it, technically, this magnificent
City, stands as it stands due to a spark and the wind!"
He was about to move on when a voice from the crowd,
forceful but measured: "Was there not a plague at
around this time?" The guide appeared to sweat instantly as he shuffled through his notes. "Ah, yes, yes. Thank
you, sir, there was, there was indeed…" The guide
quickly scanned his notes and continued. "The Plague.
A plague that had ravaged Europe for several Centuries,
wiped out vast populations, had buried its hooks into
this very land like a savage beast hunting down its prey.
That prey was you, that prey was me, that prey was anything that dared stand in its way. Royal and pauper alike
fled from its cold, deadly, clutches. Many Londoners
died, far, far more than those that perished in that fateful
fire that swept away the timber. It also swept away the
plague!" The guide nodded gratefully at the hooded
stranger as the tourists beamed, did everything but clap
the tour guide. "Let us continue, Ladies and Gentlemen,
there is so much more to see…" The huddle moved on
past the hooded stranger. He stood and then walked for
some time amongst the tourists and residents of England's metropolis. He turned down one street and then
another and pulled down his hood to reveal a young
man with a shoulder length flock of golden hair, his
eyes of bright blue, shimmering in the afternoon sun. He
smiled and walked faster as he passed the coloured
brick facades of the houses on Portobello Road. My
Love, he whispered. My Love…

*(I Will Always Love You – Whitney Houston) 1 188 714
914*

Table of Contents